# CAN A MERMAID KILL?

# CAN A MERMAID KILL?

## THOMAS B. DEWEY

**WILDSIDE PRESS**

Published by Wildside Press LLC.
www.wildsidebooks.com

# CHAPTER 1

He walked up from the surf on a long diagonal, crossing the wet beach in the early morning. The tide was out, the surf unseasonably low, so that the water itself appeared to lie far offshore; as if it had no connection with the beach, but were detached from it by some topographic lapse. From the landward viewpoint, a gull, moving toward the water on foot, seemed to vanish in a land of limbo, from which it emerged a moment later, airborne. Thus it would appear to the young woman who sat on a rock at the foot of the palisades, motionless except for the tossing of her blonde hair in the morning breeze.

The man's route brought him within ten or twelve feet of the rock and beyond it along the same line. He was about thirty years old. His build was muscular, but he was tall enough to carry it. He had brown hair, somewhat bleached by the sun, and carelessly cropped. His hands were large and supple; his large-featured face was noncommittal and relaxed, reserved rather than withdrawn. In one hand he carried an iron bar, loosely attached to his wrist by a leather strap, and from the other dangled a net sling, containing a lobster and two abalone shells. He wore faded, denim trunks and his body was burned an even, dark brown.

His eyes appeared to record the girl as a transient feature of the seascape. If she was aware of him as more than a shadow moving across her line of vision, it was not apparent. Her gaze remained fixed on the sea. He had passed some ten strides beyond her when he stopped and turned to look back at her.

"Are you all right, Miss?" he said.

The girl moved her head stiffly, not far enough to look at him. She was wearing a low-cut evening dress with narrow shoulder straps and no other wrap. Her feet, half thrust into high-heeled slippers, were turned in at the base of the rock. When she moved her face, the breeze blew strands of her hair across her eyes and forehead. A long time passed before she spoke and her thin voice nearly lost itself in the wind.

"Yes," she said, "I'm all right."

He stayed a moment longer, then nodded and went on. After a short time, the girl on the rock turned her head and watched as he climbed a knoll overgrown with ice plant, then a flight of wooden steps to a small, frame cottage set on a shelf against the palisade, beyond reach of the tides. She watched him enter and the door close behind him. There was no other dwelling in sight along this stretch of beach.

* * * *

He had the abalone out on the board behind the shack and was pounding them to edible consistency when he heard the other pounding at the door. He went through from the back and opened the door, and it was the girl from the rock.

She was carrying her shoes in one hand and shivering violently. "I guess I'm not all right, really," she said.

He stepped back to let her in and she stood huddled by the door, her eyes taking in the cottage-like, sparsely furnished room.

Then she looked at him shyly, as if embarrassed to be caught inspecting. "I didn't know how cold it would be down there," she said.

He turned to pick a long-sleeved, woolen shirt from a peg beside the door. "This time of year, in the mornings," he said.

He held the shirt while she slipped into it. Her teeth were chattering.

"I'm sorry to barge in," she said. "If I could just get warm—"

"Sure," he said. "Come back to the kitchen. It's warmer there."

She followed him to a small kitchen, where a gasoline stove was burning. There was a table, two straight-backed chairs, and a low stool. She sat on the stool in a tentative way.

"Have you had anything to eat?" he asked.

"No, I'm not hungry."

"All right. I'll be back in a couple of minutes."

Through a square window in the back door, she could see him at work over the abalone. She was still carrying her shoes in her hand. After a minute, she looked at them with curiosity, then, bending, examined a tear in the foot of her left stocking. She was forcing her feet into the shoes when he came in with the abalone.

"Feel better?" he asked.

"Yes, thanks."

She watched in trance-like detachment as he worked at the kitchen shelf. He measured coffee into a percolator, added water and set it on the stove. He broke two eggs into a bowl and whipped them, added milk and seasoning, and got out an iron skillet and put some oil in it. He opened the cooler where he had found the milk and brought out a bottle of grapefruit juice. He filled two glasses and put one on the table for her. She shook her head.

"Better drink it," he said. "May stave off the cold you deserve to get."

"I what—?"

"Sitting on the beach half naked at six in the morning."

"Oh," she said. Then, "I wasn't half naked."

The oil had begun to sputter in the pan and he dipped the abalone in the egg batter and put them in the hot oil.

"I had more clothes on than you did," she said.

"I'm used to it." He turned from the stove. "Excuse me," he said, "I didn't think. I'll put something on."

"No—it's all right. I mean, don't change your whole way of life…)

"I live alone now. I've got certain habits."

"Yes, I understand."

He went into the other room and she watched the stove. When he came back, he was wearing a sweatshirt and white dungarees.

"It may not be fancy," he said, "but it's decent."

"It's fine," she said.

He tended the sizzling abalone and turned off the heat under the coffee.

"Did you think I was indecent, sitting there in my dress?" she asked.

The question had a probing undertone and he looked annoyed. "No," he said, "I didn't think about it at all, except that you looked cold. I wondered if you were sick."

She drank some of the grapefruit juice. Swallowing, her throat labored, as if fighting an obstruction.

He poured coffee for both of them and served the abalone on pottery plates. He pulled one of the chairs around and started to sit, facing her, then got up, opened a cupboard and returned with paper napkins. "Cream and sugar?" he asked.

"No, thank you."

He sat down. She reached for the coffee eagerly, held the cup in both hands and blew over it to cool it. Her eyes looked at him through the steam, but fell away when they saw he was busy eating. "Do you get breakfast like this every day?" she asked. "I mean, do you have to go diving for it?"

"No," he said. "Sometimes. When I feel like it."

She winced as the coffee burned her mouth, but she drank it.

"Try the abalone," he said. "It's pretty good."

"I don't want to take the food out of your mouth."

"There's plenty more. The ocean's full of it."

"You're very kind."

She ate most of the abalone and drank all the coffee and juice. By then he had finished and she tried to meet his eyes and failed, though his face was not prying, but appraising; he showed more wonder than curiosity.

"You said you live alone *now*," she said. "But not always?"

"Not always."

"You mean you were married, or what?"

"Yes, I was married or what."

"I'm sorry," she said. "I guess I'm the one who should be answering questions, instead of asking them."

"I haven't asked any, have I?"

"No, you haven't asked any."

"Do you want me to?"

"No, please—I'm warm now, and well fed, thanks—abalone for breakfast! I'll go now."

But she didn't go. She sat on at the table and after a while he got up and carried the dishes to the sink. Then he went into the other room and she sat there till he came back, wearing an old, soft-brimmed hat that turned down over his face and the back of his neck.

"You're going away?" she said.

"Going to work."

"What kind of work do you do?"

"I'm a gardener. My truck is up there, at the end of the street. You must have seen it when you came down to the beach."

"I guess so. I don't remember."

She pushed at the long sleeves of the shirt and her fingers plucked at the top button, but without purpose.

"I'd better go then," she said.

"Not unless you want to," he said. "Make yourself at home. It won't warm up much outside till ten, eleven o'clock."

"Well—I didn't mean to just move in on you...) He was opening cupboards.

"If you get hungry, there's food here. A little of everything."

She looked at a stock of canned goods.

"The stove is filled and pumped," he said. "All you have to do is strike a match and turn it on."

"Well, I'm sure I won't—"

He opened the back door and took her into a passage that led to a shed-like structure attached to the house. "The facilities are in here. Primitive but clean enough. There's a shower. I don't have gas, but there's a gasoline heater. I'll light it before I go. Give it about half an hour."

She followed him back into the house, almost running to keep up with him, the square hem of the shirt flapping at her hips.

"Clean towels in here," he said, opening another cupboard. "Stay as long as you like. When you leave, be sure the stove is turned off. That's the only thing. Nobody will disturb you here. It's out of season and out of the way."

"Why do you say that?"

"What? I don't know. No special reason. You're on the beach early, not dressed for it. I guess I assumed you wanted to be alone."

"Oh, yes, that's right."

"No telephone here. Just peace and quiet and solitude."

"Sounds wonder—"

"That is except for the Old Man. But he won't be around; he knows I'm working today."

"Who is the Old Man?"

"He owns this place. I rent from him. He's quite an old man. We— talk things over."

He waited a moment for her to say something, then turned to the back door.

"You've been so nice to me," she said in a rush, "I don't know how to thank you."

He waved without turning and went out. She stood in the kitchen, listening as he lingered outside for a minute, opening the closing doors. There was the sound of his footsteps on wood. She looked out the kitchen window and watched him cross the small backyard by a boardwalk, then climb the palisade by means of a narrow path, and disappear.

She poured herself another cup of coffee and drank it, standing at the kitchen shelf. She turned on the water and rinsed the breakfast dishes, and found a dish-pan under the sink, but the water wasn't hot yet. She went to the window and looked out. There was a square wooden box at one side of the yard and she saw water reflected in it and something moving in it. She watched for a while and two slender, reddish antennae probed the air above the box. A claw rose, hooked awkwardly over the edge of the box, clung for a moment, then slipped out of sight. She shivered and turned back to the kitchen.

# CHAPTER 2

He got home at four-thirty, climbing down the palisade with a paper sack full of groceries. Approaching the shack through the backyard, he glanced at the lobster in the box and went in.

She was standing in the doorway between the kitchen and the front room, leaning against the jamb. She wore the same ankle-length dress she had come in, and his shirt and the high-heeled shoes, but she had taken off her stockings. She stood looking at the floor with her hands clasped in front of her, like a girl caught entering the dormitory after hours. A girl was what she looked like, a prematurely filled-out little girl in a rumpled party dress.

"Well, hello," he said.

He put the groceries on the shelf. He saw that the dishes had been washed and the kitchen straightened up. She was looking at him now.

"I—didn't go yet," she said.

He took a half-gallon container of milk from the sack and put it in the cooler. "I wasn't thinking too well this morning," he said. "At least I could have offered you a lift somewhere."

"No," she said. "It's because you're so kind. You didn't want to throw me out."

He put the rest of the provisions away here and there.

"Thanks for cleaning up the place," he said. "You didn't have to."

"I had to do something."

"Do you like lobster?"

"Yes, I like it very much."

"I'll clean this one and take a shower."

"What can I do? What do you want besides the lobster?"

"Well, there are some baking potatoes in the thing there, and some carrots—but you don't want to bother in that dress—" He paused, but she made no suggestion as to wardrobe, except that she could improvise an apron all right.

"I have to do something," she said.

"All right," he said. "I appreciate it."

He went into the other room and when he came back through the kitchen, carrying a small bundle of clean clothes, she had arranged a large dish towel to cover her dress and was scrubbing the potatoes at the sink. He lit the oven for her, set a kettle of water on the stove and went out.

In the bathroom, her stockings, a garter belt and a pair of negligible black panties were hanging on a string stretched above the lavatory. He looked at them for a minute, rubbed his hands over his face, then took them down and laid them on a dry towel. He got out a razor, lathered his face and shaved. When he finished, he replaced her laundry on the line and went to the kitchen for the kettle. She was peeling the carrots, awkwardly and slowly.

"What do you have for a name?" he asked.

"What? Oh—Carol. Carol Smith."

"All right, Carol. Mine is Dan."

She looked up and smiled tentatively. It was the first time she had smiled and it made her look younger, more girlish. "I like that name," she said. "Is it for Daniel?"

"No, just Dan. In the Hebrew, it means 'judge.'"

"Are you Jewish?"

"No. My father was a lawyer."

"Oh," she said. "Well—hi, Dan."

"I'll clean that lobster now."

"Do you kill it first?"

"Yes."

"Does it hurt—the lobster, I mean, when you kill it?"

"I don't know," he said. "Not for long."

She finished peeling the carrots, put them in water in a pan and set it on the stove. She went outside and stood watching for a minute or two while he worked over the lobster. Then she moved along the passage toward the bathroom, hugging the wall, as if to slip by unnoticed. When she came back, she was wearing her stockings and she had groomed her hair. She still wore his woolen shirt, but she had tucked it up loosely around her hips so that it looked less awkward.

He came in with the lobster, split it in two pieces, rinsed them at the sink, put them in a square pan and squeezed lemon juice over them. Then he did something with the oven that brought the heat up suddenly.

"I guess that's it for a few minutes," he said. "Would you like a drink?"

"Well, I—yes," she said.

"Whisky is all I have. I think there's some soda."

"Plain water, please," she said.

He opened a cupboard and took down a quart bottle of whisky. She watched without blinking while he made the highballs.

"I'm sorry, no ice," he said.

Her mouth twitched. "It's all right," she said.

"Let's go into the parlor. It's going to get pretty hot out here." He handed her a glass and led the way into the front room and fixed a place for her to sit on a square couch, covered with a gray spread and gray cushions. He brought a straight chair from the kitchen and sat where he could see both the girl and, through the window beyond the couch, the surf, and the sun setting over the long, offshore island.

The view was available to her, too, but she didn't look at it. She looked into the glass, which she held in both hands, and now and then at him, briefly, not furtively, but as if she were gauging the tenure of her welcome. She drank in sips, at frequent intervals, without savoring, as if taking medicine. "What did you do before you were a gardener?" she asked. "Before you came down here?"

"I was in business in Los Angeles. Equipment rental business."

"Equipment?"

"Tractors, bulldozers, heavy equipment."

"Oh. You were married then?"

"Yes. I sold the business in order to make the settlement."

"Then you don't have to pay alimony."

"No, no alimony."

"Did you have any children?"

"No. See the sun setting. Right about now, on a clear day, it back-lights the island, pushes it up, like floating."

She turned her face to look through the window. "It's beautiful," she said. She looked into her glass. "Then after you were divorced, you came down here? To be alone?"

Reluctantly, he pulled his vision from the window and inspected the board floor between his feet.

"Not exactly," he said. "I used to come down here with the family when I was a kid—to the town, not right to this spot. I liked it here. I had to do something, so I did gardening. I didn't especially want to be alone. It worked out that way."

She took some of her drink and he went to the kitchen. She sat, waiting, holding the glass in both hands.

* * * *

The sun was down when he served the lobster. He had brought the kitchen table in so they could eat by the window, and he lit a large, thick candle and set it in the center of the table. The candlelight softened the angular lines of her face and deepened and darkened her eyes. She had small, long-fingered hands and she used them gracefully, without affectations of elegance. She ate methodically, neither hungry nor repelled. She complimented him on the lobster.

"Not much to it," he said. "It should be fresh."

"Well, this one is fresh all right."

When they finished, it was completely dark outside. The surf rumbled, swelling and fading among the scattered phrases of their talk, giving their words the effect of tossed sea wrack.

"Thank you, that was delicious," she said.

"Would you like dessert? I have some fruit."

"No, thank you. I couldn't eat another bite."

"Are you warm enough? It cools down quickly after dark."

"I'm fine, thanks. Thanks to your shirt."

They sat in silence in the candlelight.

"I ought to go," she said. But she made no move to go.

"Is there any place I can take you?" he said. "If you don't mind riding in the truck."

"No—no, thank you."

Pretty soon he said, "You don't have any place to go, do you?"

And after a minute, she said, "No."

"You didn't even have a purse," he said.

"I had one. I lost it somewhere."

"In the morning, I'll get you some things, if you'll tell me what you want."

"You don't have to."

"It's better to have a few things," he said.

"I don't know what to say."

"It's all right. Neither would I."

They cleared the table and she helped him with the dishes. Afterward, he snuffed out the candle and they sat in the dark, watching the silver crumble of the surf against the shiny, black sand.

"Would you like to walk down on the beach?" he asked. "It's nice now."

"If you want to," she said.

"I'll get you a jacket."

He took down a leather jacket from the rack beside the door and helped her into it. She looked at her feet, showing under the long dress.

"I'd better do something," she said.

She gathered the hem of her dress and folded it upward, as high as her knees, then tied a knot in the fullness of the material at each side, so it wouldn't drop down.

"Some fancy dress, huh?" she said.

"Pretty clever," he said.

He went ahead of her down the steps and she took his hand when they reached the steep path. She moved carefully, uncertain in the dark. The sand was damp and hard and they walked southward as far as the rocky point where the cove ended. It was a clear night and there were stars, but no moon yet.

"There's a local story," he said, "that a mermaid used to hang around this point."

"A mermaid? Oh, a girl with a fish tail."

"She would sit up there in the sun and comb the seaweed out of her hair and develop a tan. So naturally, some of the guys on the beach tried to get acquainted, but she was shy and nobody could get to first base. It wasn't that she was so beautiful, but—something different.

"So one of the guys, who was a pretty good skin diver, figured out that she might be more available in her own element, and he decided to follow her when she left the rock. He got his rig on and his gear and he was fooling around about fifty yards offshore, watching the mermaid on the rock, and when she hit the water, he took a dive."

The girl waited, then said, "Did he find out where she lived?"

"Nobody knows," he said. "He never came back. There were theories. Some of the guys said she probably had a cave or something down there and he had gone in and couldn't get out. Some figured that most fish don't live any particular place and maybe she had taken off, heading way out, and the skin diver had kept after her till he ran out of air and couldn't get back, or the sharks had gotten him."

"Didn't they try to find him?"

"Oh sure. They went all out, but—nothing. But the mermaid came back, as usual, almost every day over a period of time."

"Did they learn anything from her?"

"Well, no. She didn't talk or anything and it was impossible to get close to her. She was very shy, and quick. Anybody got too close, she'd be in the water and gone. They tried various things, but nothing worked out. Finally they made a total effort. They got up a string of skin divers and boats and set up stations. When the mermaid took off, one diver went after her, and he was rigged so they could follow his trail. When he gave the signal, the next diver picked up where he left off, and so on."

"Pretty smart," the girl said.

"Yeah. They followed her to the island and past it and about forty miles out to sea, and then they ran out of divers and had to give up. Her last reported bearing was toward Hawaii."

"She never came back to the rock again?"

After a minute, he said, "Once, quite a long time later."

"And what happened?"

"Well, she showed up on the rock and some people notified the local law. After all, that skin diver had never been accounted for and if there had been any foul play, the cops wanted to know about it. So they plotted a little strategy. There were half a dozen of them, in plain clothes. They were going to take her in and the only excuse they had was a charge of indecent exposure. Because, naturally, she didn't wear any clothes and her—uh—femaleness was pretty obvious."

"You mean she would sit around on the beach half naked?"

He chuckled. "I'm sorry about that," he said.

"I didn't mean to interrupt. What happened?"

"The cops kind of spread out and a couple of them, without getting too close, got the mermaid's attention and started talking to her through a portable loud-speaking system. Of course, she didn't understand the words, as far as anybody could tell, but she seemed kind of fascinated, and while the cops with the horn were holding her attention, the rest of them threw a dragnet around the rocks. They had a skin diver, too, just offshore, under water. They were closing in on her pretty good when she sensed trouble and made for the water. The skin diver managed to get hold of her and the others jumped in, clothes and all, to help. Later, they said it was like trying to catch a porpoise with your bare hands. They took an awful beating on the rocks."

He stopped. The girl stared at him.

"Well," she said, "what happened? Did they catch her?"

"Oh, no. She got away."

He took her hand and they started back toward the house, walking along the edge of the surf.

"Wait a minute," she said, tugging at his hand. "You can't stop there. Is that all there is?"

"Just about. Not much of a story, I guess. There's a moral to it, though."

After a moment, she sighed. "All right, what's the moral?"

"There are stranger fish in the sea than ever get caught."

"That's some moral."

"Well, it's all I've got."

"I want to know what happened to her, the mermaid."

"What about the poor skin diver?"

"Him, too, but after all, he asked for it."

"I guess we'll never know. It's likely there's no such thing as a mermaid."

"You're crazy."

"I guess so."

Her hand tightened in his and she halted. "Who's that? Somebody's coming."

He looked at the lean shadow angling across the beach toward the shack. "It's all right," he said. "It's the Old Man."

"Do you want him to know about me?"

"What about you?"

"That I'm here, I mean."

"I don't care, it's up to you. You don't have to worry about him. He's all right. I'd trust him with anything I own."

The Old Man had stopped and they walked over and met him at the foot of the path.

"Hello, Sol."

"Good evening, boy," the Old Man said, in a dry, old man's voice. He looked at the girl. "My name isn't really Sol; that's a nickname for Solomon, which isn't my name either."

"Carol," Dan said, "this is Mister Baumgarten. Jack Baumgarten—Carol."

"It's a pleasure, Miss," the Old Man said.

"Hello, Mister Baumgarten," she said.

"He calls me Solomon because I'm old enough to be," Mr. Baumgarten said.

"Come on up," Dan said.

"Oh, no—I was just taking a late stroll."

"So were we. Come on," Dan said, "unless you don't feel up to the climb."

The Old Man sighed. "Always the young challenge," he murmured. "Shall I go first?"

"Please," Carol said.

Mr. Baumgarten started up the path and Dan, taking Carol's hand, climbed after him.

\* \* \* \*

When the Old Man rose to leave, Dan saw that the girl was asleep. He opened a blanket that lay folded on the couch, and covered her. Then he went outside with the Old Man.

They descended the steps and the path in silence. On the sand, the Old Man paused.

"Don't ask me," Dan said. "She's there. Do you mind?"

"Who would mind?" Mr. Baumgarten said. "A man is a man."

"It's not like that," Dan said. "She just turned up."

"She's a pretty thing."

"I don't know. I guess so."

They walked out on the sand toward the surf. The Old Man was taking his leave when he turned back as an afterthought.

"Almost forgot the big news," he said. "You were in the village today?"

"No, I worked south. What happened?"

"Big excitement. A prominent playboy citizen, Benedict—"

"The old Benedict family?"

"Yes. The rich, ne'er-do-well son—middle-aged by now. Somebody shot him, last night or early this morning. Big conversational rumpus. Opinion divided as to whether he deserved it or not. Popular man in some quarters, disreputable in others."

"No idea who did it?"

"Apparently not. Air full of speculation, lists of names, girlfriends, men friends, debtors, even relatives. Seems he has an alcoholic sister dependent on him for support."

"She's one of my customers—Saturday mornings. I never met her brother."

"The story's full of clichés, police baffled, juicy scuttlebutt. In the city, it would be a news editor's dream come true. Different handling down here; we don't have murder. Isn't feasible. The exceptions are fairly splashy."

A swirl of surf engulfed Dan's right shoe. He kicked it away.

"Well," he said, "so it goes."

"Ah yes. Goodnight, thanks for the game."

"I'll beat you yet, one of these days."

"Undoubtedly."

"Goodnight, Solly."

He watched the Old Man out of sight, then stayed a while, brooding over the incoming surf, before turning back to the path.

The girl woke, startled, when he entered, and gazed at him with her small face sandwiched between her upthrust shoulders, bulky in the big jacket.

"Didn't mean to scare you," he said. "I walked out with the Old Man."

"It's all right," she said. "I mean, you didn't scare me."

"Let's fix that up to make you comfortable."

He helped her off the couch and she stood, blinking, clutching the blanket in both arms, while he removed the cover and cushions from the couch to reveal a sheeted bed.

"These are clean," he said. "I got them from the laundry yesterday and changed them after I got up this morning."

"But what about you?"

"I've got a sleeping bag. Don't worry about me."

"But I can't just move in on you."

He looked at her and her eyes fell. She hugged the blanket.

"Thank you," she said. "I guess—I don't know what to do."

"You'll feel better after a good night's sleep."

He took the blanket from her and spread it on the couch.

"I'll turn on a light in the bathroom for you," he said. "I fixed the heater, so the water is still hot."

She followed him through the kitchen and outside and waited while he made a light in the bathroom.

When she came back, he was opening a sleeping bag on the floor, across the room from the couch. He had moved the table back to the kitchen and there was a clear area between the head of the couch and the window. She stood by the window, looking out.

"Thank you," she said, "I don't know what I would have done. Maybe tomorrow—"

"I don't have any pajamas to offer you," he said. "I put another blanket on the bed. I think you'll be warm enough."

"I'll be fine."

"In the morning, I'll get you some things. Do you want to go with me, to pick them out?"

"No, please."

"What size are you?"

"What size? Oh, I wear nine hose, thirty-four blouse and seven dress. Other things I wear are the smallest. 'Petite' they call it."

"Okay, little Carol. I'll let you get into bed now."

He left the room, going out through the kitchen. The girl turned from the window, took off the heavy jacket and then the sweater, and hung them on the rack beside the door. She loosened the knots at the sides of her raised skirt and shook out the hem. The material was badly wrinkled. She hesitated a moment, then stooped, found the hem and pulled the dress off over her head. She wore panties and a half-bra, a garter belt, stockings and shoes. She shook out the dress again, laid it across the bed, sat down and took off her shoes and stockings and the garter belt. She dropped them in a small pile on the floor and got into bed. After a minute, she began to cry silently.

When Dan returned, she appeared to be asleep and he crawled into the bedroll without speaking.

# CHAPTER 3

In the morning, the girl was sleeping. He rose quietly and stowed the bedroll away. He wrote a note, anchored it with a salt shaker on the kitchen table, and left the house without waking her.

He stopped for breakfast at a roadside cafe on the highway south of town. It was early and he was the only customer. The operator of the cafe was a large, hearty woman of forty-five, named Estelle.

The morning paper from the city was lying on the counter and he glanced through it while she prepared his eggs and bacon. There was no news that caught his interest. Estelle brought his breakfast and refilled his coffee cup.

"There you go, Danny boy," she said.

Halfway through the meal, he said, "You're a good girl in the kitchen, Estelle. You ought to get married."

"In general?" she said. "Or specifically?"

"In general."

"And do all this work for free? I don't think so."

"You could marry some rich guy."

"I could? You know of one?"

"Well, I could look around."

"Thanks, but to tell you the truth, I guess I'm just as well off this way. I only have one boss. Me."

"I know what you mean."

Pretty soon she said, "Besides, these rich guys don't seem to be such a bargain. Like that Freddie Benedict, for instance. Look what happened to him."

"You think a woman shot him?"

"Who else? Why would a man shoot him?"

"I didn't know him."

"Well, I mean he wasn't a queer, that I know of. He liked girls."

"Lots of girls?"

"As many as possible, I guess."

"Did he pay?"

"How would I know?"

"Excuse me."

"I guess he had his points, for the kind of guy he was. I hear he even did a certain amount of good. And he had a way with women."

"And all that money."

"All that money. More coffee?"

"Thanks. What do they think about it—the cops?"

"Well, the last I heard, they thought it was probably some girl he had set up and she didn't like the way things went, so she shot him and left town."

He drank some of the coffee.

"Do they know of a particular visitor he had that night?"

"He always had visitors. Who kept track?"

"Local girl, they think?"

"I don't know. They're checking out alibis. I doubt if it was a local girl. Probably somebody from L.A. She's probably in Mexico by now."

He finished the coffee and paid his check.

"Okay, Estelle," he said, "I'll keep my eyes open."

"Sure, Danny."

He left the cafe, got into his truck and drove south on the highway.

* * * *

He was working along the oleander hedge on the upper slope, when Mrs. Fairweather came out of the house and climbed the stone steps. She was a stringy, ageless woman, with brown, sinewy hands and an expression of secret amusement.

"We're out early this morning," she said.

He was pruning the oleanders, and tying back the sprawling stalks to bring the plants erect. "Yes, ma'am," he said. "I'm hooked on the inspirational writings of Benjamin Franklin."

Mrs. Fairweather laughed and inspected his work surreptitiously. "I thought, if you have time," she said, "we might repot some of the chrysanthemums."

"Sure," he said, "plenty of time."

She lingered a moment, as if she had something more to say, then turned back to the house.

Later, they were working over the pots, loading the new pots with mulch and transferring the chrysanthemum plants from smaller pots, methodically, one by one.

"What do you think of our big sensation?" Mrs. Fairweather asked.

"Sensation? Oh, the murder. I don't know. I haven't thought much about it."

"Our family was quite close to the Benedicts for years," she said, "but I never knew this Freddie to speak of. I remember when he was a toddler. Funny how some people turn out."

"Yes," he said.

Mrs. Fairweather worked busily over one of the pots.

"I try never to gossip," she said. "It's not becoming to an old woman. Oops—we forgot to cover the hole in this one."

Dan took the pot, picked up a fragment of clay pottery, dug into the mulch and worked the fragment into position over the hole in the bottom of the pot.

"However," Mrs. Fairweather said, "I can't stop thinking. It's odd— the Benedicts were upright, church-going citizens; I mean, the senior Benedicts. Never drank, smoked, very stern people. The children were brought up quite strictly. Now, the daughter, I understand, is an alcoholic, and the son, well…)

Dan said nothing and after a while, Mrs. Fair-weather said, "Do you think that's odd? Or is it what we ought to expect? We're told, by modern standards, that bringing children up too strictly, repressing them—suppressing?—is likely to boomerang. What do you think?"

Reluctantly, Dan said, "I don't know. I guess it isn't that simple. There must be a lot of people who are brought up strictly who don't turn into alcoholics and—so forth. Of course, if you put a dog in a tight cage, and abuse him and frustrate him, he will get mean and un-doglike."

"But a dog is not a person."

"True. But we get just about the same results when we put criminals in prison."

"Well, I guess we have to have prisons. But you can't—if you have children—you can't just bring up your daughters on gin and whisky, in order to keep them from becoming alcoholics; and you can't provide your son with all the girls he wants, just so he won't be frustrated."

"No, you can't do that."

"So what can you do?"

"Whoa! Don't ask me."

"All right. But under that laconic exterior of yours, I sense a philosopher. Am I wrong?"

"I don't know about that, but how to bring up children is not a philosophical question. It's more of a practical question, and I never had any experience." Picking up two of the freshly filled pots, he escaped into the shade of a lath house. Mrs. Fairweather turned to another chore.

He was dumping the last of the cuttings and sweepings into the truck when she came from the house, bringing a check.

"I nearly forgot it was payday," she said sternly. "You didn't remind me."

"I never do," he said.

"Are you against money, too?" she said.

"Money too?"

"I mean, you're against prisons and cruelty to animals and having children—"

"No, ma'am. I just said I didn't have any practical experience bringing up children. I hear that the trick is to leave them alone when they're infants and put the clamps on slowly."

"Now you're talking. What kind of clamps?"

He shrugged. "I don't know. Responsibility—"

"That's the nub of it, isn't it?" she said. "Responsibility to what?"

He grinned at her, folding the check into his shirt pocket. "Can we hold that over for the next meeting?" he said.

"Okay," she said. "Give it some thought."

She turned abruptly and walked back to the house and he swung into his truck and got started. He turned north, toward town, but after a short distance, pulled off to one side and sat beside the road for a minute. Then he made a U-turn across the highway and headed south again. He drove for several miles and turned into a small shopping center. He went into a market, bought a few supplies and cashed Mrs. Fairweather's check. Then he walked a few doors down the street and went into a women's dress shop called *In the Mode*.

\* \* \* \*

The girl struggled out of sleep as if drugged. There was no clock in the house, but the unshadowed sand and blue water showed it was nearly noon. She sat for a long time, on the edge of the bed, looking down at the beach. She sat doubled forward, her arms crossed under her breasts, as if in pain. Then she found her shoes in the small pile she had built beside the bed and put them on. She took down the heavy shirt beside the door and put that on over her brassiere and panties.

In the kitchen, she found the note on the table and read it several times, as if it were in code and had to be deciphered. Finally, she left it where she had found it and went outside. She was gone a long rime. When she came back to the kitchen, she read the note again, then lit a burner on the stove, using several matches, and put water on to boil. She found a can of coffee and measured some into a pot, moving with heavy listlessness, pausing often to gaze at her hands, or at the shelf, or floor. When she had set the coffee pot on the stove, suddenly, for no apparent reason, her hands began to shake. She looked at them with a kind of wonder, then bent forward, folded her arms over her stomach and rested her head against the kitchen shelf. She remained in that position for a long time, as earlier on the bed.

When she straightened up, she opened a high cupboard and peered into it, pushed the stool into position, climbed onto it and took down the bottle of whisky. She set it on the shelf and got down a glass and took the cap off the bottle. Then she stood stiffly at the shelf, her fingernails digging at the linoleum top, and stared at the bottle. After a while, with the same plodding heaviness, she replaced the cap, put the bottle back on the shelf and put the unused glass away. She held up her hands and looked at them and they were still shaking, but not as violently as before.

She found a bottle of fruit juice in the cooler, poured a glass of it and drank slowly, leaning against the shelf. When the water boiled on the stove, she filled the coffee pot and stood quietly near it until it had dripped through. Then she filled a cup and took it into the front room. She stood at the window, drinking the coffee and looking out at the beach. A tall, lean-shanked man walked with brisk, bird-like strides on the wet sand. He was barefoot and his trousers were rolled above his knees. As she watched, he veered unexpectedly toward the palisades, as if to approach the house. She moved back from the window quickly and some of the coffee spilled on her hand. She shifted the cup and shook the hand vigorously.

"Jesus!" she said through her teeth.

She sat down on the bed and drank the rest of the coffee. When it was gone, she set the cup on the floor.

"Jesus," she said quietly. "Oh, Jesus."

She lay down on the bed and drew her knees up to her breasts. After a minute, she pulled one of the blankets up to her shoulders. She lay still for several minutes, her eyes half closed against the sunlight coming through the window. Then slowly, deliberately, she pulled the blanket over her head and face.

"Oh Jesus, Jesus, Jesus," she said. "Oh God."

\* \* \* \*

He climbed down from the cliff, the market sack in one arm and the larger package, bulky and awkward, in the other. He let himself in at the back door, saw that the girl had been up, and put the sack on the shelf. He took the larger package into the front room. She was propped on her hands in bed, wearing his shirt.

"Feel better?" he said.

Her mouth twitched in a forced smile. "I'm fine, thanks."

He put the package on the bed near her feet. "I hope these fit all right."

"You shouldn't have."

"Probably not, but I got to thinking—what if we'd have company?"

Her eyes moved to fix on him.

"You mean like Mister Baumgarten?"

"Well—him, too."

She reached for the package, stretching, and drew it by the string within reach.

"Thank you," she said. "If I could find my purse, I could pay you."

He had started out of the room, but stopped in the kitchen doorway.

"Where do you think you lost your purse?" he asked.

"I don't know."

"I mean, what part of town were you in? Were you just walking along, or did you leave it in a car somewhere?"

"No, not in a car."

He lingered, not looking at her, but waiting pointedly, as if this question must be answered. She stopped clawing at the string on the package and put her fist to her mouth. Then, as if realizing the gesture was absurd, she thrust her balled fist into the bed beside her thigh. She spoke from a crouch, looking toward the sunlit window, as if at any moment she might spring through it and disappear.

"I'm not too clear about it," she said. "You see, there was this party—and I—well, I guess I got a little tight. And so—it got very late and I had to go out—go for a walk, and I was walking along the cliff and it wasn't daylight yet. So I saw this path down to the beach and decided to go down there. And up at the top there's a lot of bushes—along the street there—with thorns—"

"Bougainvillea," he said.

"Yes, bougainvillea. So I couldn't see very well, and I was feeling around for where the path started down, and I dropped my purse. Well, I thought maybe it went over the cliff. And then I thought it probably went in those bushes—in the bougain-stuff—and I tried to find it, but there were all those thorns. Anyway, there wasn't anything in it except money and I didn't expect to need it on the beach. I thought I could find it after it was light, when I came back up...)

Her head dropped between her arms. She was panting, as if the explanation had exhausted her.

He moved toward the bed, then stopped. "Okay," he said. "If you want to look over the things—maybe something needs changing."

She nodded wearily and he left the room.

When he returned, she had opened the package and the things he had brought were scattered over the couch. She was trying on a yellow blouse and from the waist down, she was naked. She glanced at him without shyness.

"It's lovely," she said.

"Excuse me," he said, and started out.

"What for?" she said. "Oh."

She looked down at herself, then, calmly, she picked up a pair of new white panties and stepped into them. "I'm sorry," she said. "I didn't think." Among the things on the bed were two skirts, one light colored, the other dark, and a print dress with a square bodice and flaring skirt. She picked up the lighter skirt, stepped into it and snapped it at the waist, tucking the blouse in smooth, pulled the zipper up and turned this way and that, twisting to examine the fit. Then, as if remembering he was still there, she smiled and performed a mock pirouette, but gracefully, and struck a pose.

"Thank you, sir," she said. "They're perfect."

"Good."

"I'm sorry," she said. "I was careless. I was—used to go to a nudist camp. With my sister."

"No problem here," he said. "It was only that I forgot to knock."

She went to him, put her hands on his shoulders and kissed him quickly.

"I'm lucky," she said. "I'll pay you back. I promise."

"Don't worry about paying. I didn't get any shoes because that's tricky. Maybe we could go down the road and find some. Maybe this evening."

She stood with her hands at her sides and nodded soberly. "All right. If you want."

"I brought some things for lunch. I'll have to get back to work."

"Let me fix it."

She made a lunch of cold cuts, boiled peas, and a carrot and raisin salad. She was quite animated during the preparations and while they ate, but just before he left she turned brooding and listless again. She was sitting on the bed, fingering the new clothes he had brought, and she said, "You must be pretty well-known around here."

"Hardly at all," he said, laughing.

"I mean, you said you came down when you were a boy."

"I was just a summer visitor. The place has changed. I've lived to myself on the beach here. Practically never go to town."

"I was just thinking—in those stores—they must have thought it was land of funny, the things they were selling you."

"I don't know. I didn't go to the village."

"Oh."

"There's a shopping center down the road."

"Why? Why did you go down there, instead of into town? Because you might be embarrassed?"

He frowned at her insistence. "No," he said. "I was working down that way. It was handy."

"Oh. Well, thank you."

"I have to go now," he said. "I'll be back before dark."

"All right," she said.

He climbed to the street. His truck was parked at the dead end of a wide street that led from the highway to the top of the palisades. On one side of the street, the land dropped into a deep arroyo that opened into a cove beyond his shack. The other side was a vacant, level lot that had been subdivided long before, but never developed. A dirt road ran along the top of the palisades for a short distance and ended. Between the highway and the palisades were street signs for roads that had never been built. A row of tall palms, shaggy and unkempt, grew along the street across from the arroyo. Bougainvillea had been planted along the top of the cliff, bordering the dirt road. Infrequently tended, the sparsely blooming stalks spread at random, forming an impenetrable barrier, except where a path had been cut to give access to the beach. The bougainvillea grew thick on both sides of the path, which began about seventy-five feet from his own private route to the shack, and fifty feet from where his truck was parked.

He took a pair of long-handled pruning shears from the truck. A black and white patrol car from the sheriff's local station swung into the street, made a U-turn and parked, facing the highway. Dan began to prune the tips of the bougainvillea stalks where they hung over the curb and street. He pruned slowly, working from some distance beyond the path back toward the truck. At the other end of the street, the patrol car hovered.

He had a long clutter of clippings along the curb, when he laid the shears down and went to the truck. He returned with a broom and a large square of burlap sacking. He spread the sacking on the street and swept the clippings into it. The patrol car lingered as he picked up the shears and began pruning again at the mouth of the path, working around the south lip as far as the first steep descent, where the bougainvillea straggled out and gave way to dense, green ice plant. He was working along the other lip, climbing, glancing now and then at the patrol car, when he found the purse.

It was just below the brow of the descent, where the path made its first downward swoop—near enough to have been dropped. It was a small, beaded evening bag with a gold chain for a handle, and it lay in a nest of ivy under a web of flowering bougainvillea. He left it there and went on pruning.

By the time he had worked his way to the end of the street and the shadow of his truck, the patrol car was gone. He put the shears away, returned and swept up the cuttings, moving more quickly now. He gathered the corners of the sacking, lifted the bundle to his shoulder and took it, with the broom, to the truck. Then he went back and picked up the purse and, without opening it, returned by his own path to the shack.

The girl was at the kitchen sink, with a towel covering her new skirt, washing the dishes. He laid the purse on the shelf.

"You found it," she said.

"Up by the path."

She dried her hands on the towel and reached for the purse. "I'll pay you for the clothes."

"No time now, I have to go."

"Well, thank you again."

He started out.

"Oh, wait a minute!" she said.

She ran into the other room and returned. "You forgot your hat."

He reached for it, but she evaded his hand and set the hat on his head, somewhat fussily, adjusting the broad brim to her own satisfaction.

"There," she said. "That afternoon sun isn't good for you on the bare head."

He smiled, nodding. "You are right, thanks. I'll be back about five o'clock."

"All right," she said.

She went to the back door and watched him out of sight. Then she turned to the shelf, opened the evening bag and shook out the contents. It made a minute clutter on the linoleum. She culled out a crumpled, red-stained tissue and threw it into a sack under the sink. There remained a linen and lace handkerchief without a monogram, a small emery board, a lipstick and flat compact, and a coin purse. She opened it and shook out a few coins and some wadded currency. She sorted and smoothed out the bills. There were half a dozen bills of small denominations, and one other, which she pushed to one side. This one had a value of one thousand dollars.

Carefully, item by item, she refilled her purse, leaving the thousand-dollar bill on the shelf. She took the purse into the other room and put it on the bed among the new clothes. She went back to the kitchen, picked up the thousand-dollar bill and a match from the box on the stove. Holding the bill over the sink, she set fire to it and watched it burn, turning it this way and that, shifting her fingertip grasp from corner to corner, until only a fragment of uncharred paper remained. She crumbled the black residue, emptied the dishwater over it and watched it bubble down the drain. She scrubbed the sink with cleanser, washed her hands and dried them and, taking the towel from around her waist, began to dry the dishes.

# CHAPTER 4

On the outskirts of the town, he drove away from a nursery, parked in front of a small coffee shop and went inside. En route, he picked up a copy of the afternoon city paper from the outdoor, rack. He ordered a cup of coffee, to go, and waited while a girl filled a paper container. He took it and the paper to the truck and sat drinking the coffee and looking through the paper. When the coffee was gone, he set the container aside on top of the folded paper and drove on toward town.

\* \* \* \*

At four o'clock, he was completing the brick terrace of a hillside home between the highway and the beach. He was laying the brick dry, in square sections formed of redwood 2 x 4s. He worked without apparent hurry, but with such economy of movement that his progress was rapid. The terrace was the highest of three levels comprising the lot and could be approached either by a winding path that led from the garage along one side of the house, or from the house itself by way of the kitchen or breakfast room. The kitchen windows were open and over the quiet thudding of his work came sounds: the slam of a refrigerator door, the rush of water from a tap, ice clinking in a glass. A woman's heels clicked busily.

"Starting early today, darling?" she said.

A man's voice answered with a slight drawl. "On special days, I start early. This is in the nature of a wake."

"How touching. Dear old Freddie. Make me one, I'll help celebrate."

There was the sound of the refrigerator again, more clinking ice, more water.

"Tell me," the woman said, "why would a man choose to kill himself in this particular way? With whisky?"

"Do you worry?" he said. "I'm worth quite a lot more dead than alive."

"I keep thinking of that."

"Let me give you a bit of advice. When you get around to it, don't use your own gun or one of mine. Borrow one. It's like the credit system; better not to use your own money."

"Oh shut up," she said. And after a minute she said, "One thing I'm sorry about poor, dear Freddie Benedict. I'm sorry it wasn't some solid, respectable hausfrau who shot him, instead of one of those—monsters he used to import."

"How do you know it wasn't some solid hausfrau?" he said. "Where were you last night, for instance?"

"You dirty bastard," the woman said.

Her heels went away, staccato diminuendo.

The kitchen door opened and the man came out to the terrace. He had gray hair and a soft-looking face, though handsome, and was dressed in knee-length shorts and a Hawaiian sport shirt. His face bore a look of fixed geniality. "Looks great," he said, inspecting the new terrace floor. "Deserves a bonus."

"I'm glad it's all right," Dan said.

He had finished the job and was gathering up his tools.

"How about collecting the bonus right now?" the man said. "Let me fix you a drink."

"No thanks," Dan said. "Not today."

The man looked at him somberly. "Are you married, Danny?" he said.

"No," Dan said.

The man shook his head. "That's a shame," he said. "A dirty, goddam shame."

"Anything you say," Dan said, and took the tools by way of the side path to where his truck was parked in front of the garage. When he went back to the terrace for one last survey, the man was leaning against the corner of the house, brooding into his glass.

"A dirty shame," he said. "Freddie Benedict wasn't married either, and look what happened to him."

Dan wiped his hands on his jeans.

"I guess so," he said. "I didn't know Mister Benedict."

The man shook his head again. "In a way," he said, "you missed quite a lot, not knowing Freddie. In another way, you didn't."

"Uh-huh," Dan said.

The man smiled brightly. "Pretty profound, huh?" he said. "Not bad on one drink. Come around about eight o'clock. I'll be real profound."

"Well, I guess that's all for this time," Dan said. "See you next week."

"Okay."

Dan went away around the house.

\* \* \* \*

He parked the truck at the dead end of the empty street. The sun was hanging low over the island and he sat for a few minutes, watching the sunset display. The dramatic sky dominated the view, so that the darkening water seemed incidental, merely a background.

He left the truck and walked along the cliff edge northward, hesitating at his own path. He glanced down at the shack, which showed no sign of life, then went on. Just beyond the path, he cut away from the cliff to follow the southern rim of the arroyo towards the highway. The ravine grew shallower in that direction and at length he crossed it by a dipping trail worn through sagebrush and scrub growth. From the other side, he approached a low, walled, Spanish style house of white plaster and red tile, that sat alone between the highway and the beach.

An antique bell hung beside an iron gate and he rang it three times, with a measured pause after the first and second rings, and then he opened the gate and went in. Jack Baumgarten was sitting in a flagstone patio with a highball glass on the table beside him.

The patio was colorful and verdant. Fuchsias and geraniums in wire baskets and pots hung from brackets on the old wall, and ivy climbed thickly among them. There was a round pool in the center of the space. Two fat, nondescript cats drowsed on its broad rim. There were fish in the pool, but it was built in the form of a well, so the fish were inaccessible to the cats except by total immersion. A glow of lingering sunlight highlighted the top of the wall.

Dan sat down on the pool rim beside one of the cats.

"Greetings," the Old Man said. "Drink?"

"Thanks."

He waited, stroking the cat, while the Old Man went into the house and returned with a highball.

"Salud," Dan said. He glanced around the richly traditional setting. "How did a guy named Baumgarten light on a place like this?"

The Old Man chuckled. His lean, brown face was seamed, and when he laughed the lines deepened and radiated from his eyes across his temples.

"On my mother's side," he said, "we're Spanish."

The last of the sunlight vanished from the wall.

"We have an old, more or less honorable heritage in Spain," Baumgarten said. "Have one ancestor, served as legal adviser to none other than Torquemada himself—sub rosa, naturally. A right-thinking man, my ancestor; tried to arrest that madness—got himself liquidated for his pains. But privately, not in public; something of a break in those days."

He coughed lightly, apologetically.

"My great aunt, Dolores Lopez—beautiful girl, lusty—artist's model—had twelve children by five fathers. I have a good many pictures of her—show you sometime. Every damn one of 'em, she's gravid! Single-handed population explosion. Gorgeous woman—mother of the race."

They drank for a while, in silence, in the gathering darkness.

"Listen," Dan said explosively, so that the cats blinked. "Did you know this guy—Freddie Benedict?"

The Old Man replied after a moment, his voice wary. "In passing," he said. "Did some business with him once, traded some properties. But just business—met him in the escrow office, shook hands. I knew him well enough to say hello on the street."

"No better than that."

"That's about it. Pleasant enough fellow, but hard to talk to, as I remember. There's a kind of preoccupation takes over in a dedicated voluptuary. I've noticed that."

"How much of a voluptuary was he?"

"Don't know. Shouldn't have mentioned it. Hearsay."

Dan finished his drink and set the empty glass on the table. The brief twilight had faded and the Old Man's face and the cats and the patio furnishings were breaking into fragmented silhouettes.

"Got to go," Dan said. "I told her I'd be home before dark."

The Old Man was silent.

"Do you ever get lonely?" Dan asked. "Living alone like this?"

"Sometimes, yes. No sign of weakness to be lonely. It's in how you take it. Depression in a reasonably healthy mind is self-indulgence. Melancholy is legitimate."

Dan got up, moving toward the gate, and the Old Man rose to follow.

"I'd like to help you, if possible," the Old Man said. "You're still young, been through a normal, hermitic interlude. Maybe one way to break out is as good as another. One thing, though—well, the hell with it."

"Go ahead," Dan said. "Give it to me."

"I always tried to steer clear of crystallizing things," the Old Man said. "Impulse nigh irresistible. I coined one aphorism in my life—think I did; form of a paradox. Anyway, here it is, useful or not: Permanence is fleeting."

Dan rattled the iron latch. "Permanence is fleeting," he said. "I like it."

"Come and see me any time," the Old Man said. "I sleep only now and then."

"All right, thanks." He opened the gate, then turned back. "I owe you some explanation," he said, "but I don't know how...)

"No," the Old Man said.

"Well, thanks for the drink."

"Any time, Dan. *Hasta la vista.*"

"*Vaya con Yahweh*, Jack."

He walked away quickly and after a few moments the gate clanged shut.

* * * *

There were no lights in the shack and he hesitated at the door, then opened it quickly and went in. One of the stove burners was lighted and there was the sound of boiling water.

"Hello?" he called. "Carol?"

"Yes, in here."

He found her sitting on the bed by the window, a glass in her hands. She was wearing the same skirt she had first tried on, but she had changed her blouse. She had gathered her hair tightly to form a ponytail and her profile in the faint light of the window was flagrantly girlish.

"I'm sorry," he said. "I forgot to show you about the lamps."

"I'm not afraid of the dark," she said. She held up the glass. "I made myself a drink. Is it all right?"

"I don't know. I don't know how good a bartender you are."

"Well—I'll make one for you, and then you'll know. How's that?"

"Fine, but suppose I take a shower first? Do you want some light now?"

"No. I mean, if you don't need it, I like it this way."

"Okay, I won't be long." He went to the wardrobe in the rear corner of the room and took fresh clothes from it. "This time it's true," he said. "I was late tonight because I went to see the Old Man for a few minutes."

"You don't have to explain to me," she said, "but thanks anyway."

"I'll be with you pronto."

"I'll wait, señor."

He went out through the kitchen with the clothes over his arm.

Returning, he stopped to light a lamp in the kitchen. Carol came to the door and her eyes went wide.

"Well," she said, "when you dress for a drink, you go all the way, don't you?"

He was wearing a full suit of clothes, hard shoes, a white shirt and a necktie.

"I thought some strange man had walked in," she said.

"Come on," he said, "I'm not a total slob. Not yet. Once in a while I put on a suit, go to dinner—"

"I didn't mean you were a slob."

"How about that drink?"

"Coming right up."

He went into the other room. From the shelf in the wardrobe, he took down a strongbox. It wasn't locked. He opened it and took out some currency, closed the box and replaced it on the shelf. He struck a match and was about to light a lamp, changed his mind, shook out the match and threw it away, leaving the room dark except for the glow from the kitchen. She came in with the glasses and they sat in the half dark, she on the bed, he on the one chair.

"I don't have any dinner ready for you," she said, "because I didn't know what you'd want, and then it got dark."

"I thought we could go get you a pair of shoes and have dinner somewhere."

"Oh. Where would we go? Are the stores open tonight?"

"Friday, yes. We could go down to the shopping center, or on down the coast a ways."

"That would be fun. I've never been south of here."

"Never been to San Diego?"

"No. Oh, I forgot—just once, I went through it. I was in Tijuana once."

"Was it fun?"

"I can hardly remember. I was only about twelve years old. I remember I bought something—jewelry, an Indian thing. Very pretty and it didn't cost much. I still have it somewhere."

"This is a very good drink."

"It was nothing, really. How was the Old—Mister Baumgarten?"

"Just fine, but he usually is."

"How old is he?"

"About seventy-five, I think. He's in great shape."

"He lives all alone?"

"With a couple of cats, in a big old Spanish house. It's up there on the other side of the arroyo."

She turned her glass in her two hands. "He likes you," she said.

Dan shrugged. "I don't know. I like him."

"Yes," she said. "He loves you—like a son."

"How can you tell this?"

"I don't know. It's just something a person can feel. Maybe a woman can see it where a man wouldn't—wouldn't notice, I mean."

They finished their drinks in silence.

"Well," he said, getting up, "let's go get something to put on your petite feet."

She glanced at the foot of the bed, where she had made a neat stack of the new clothes.

"Will we be going to a fancy restaurant?" she asked.

"Not exactly," he said. "There isn't anything very fancy in that direction. We can go in the other direction, if you'd rather."

"Oh no. I just wondered if I should change to a dress."

"You look fine from here."

"Yeah," she said. "In the dark, at ten paces."

"You might want to put on a sweater."

"I think so."

\* \* \* \*

He took her hand to help her up the path to the street. In the other hand, she clutched the small, beaded bag. On top of the cliff, she held back, catching her breath, and looked around curiously, as if she had never seen the area before, or as if she had been shut away for a long time and was trying to remember how it had been.

"Whoo!" she said.

"I would install a lift," he said soberly, "but it's a nice workout."

"Yes indeed."

"Will you wait while I bring up the car?"

"Knock it off now. Let's go."

At the truck, she made a gesture of admiration. "It's beautiful."

"Damn right," he said. "It's one of the few things I saved out of the domestic mess."

The step was too high for her in the tight skirt and she pulled it up above her knees. He boosted her into the cab. When he got in beside her, she had adjusted her skirt over her knees and was leaning forward slightly.

"It's wonderful," she said. "It's so high! You can look down on all the people."

"A built-in feature," he said.

She clung to the door as he started it and swung in a slow U-turn toward the highway.

\* \* \* \*

The shopping center wasn't crowded and he parked outside a women's shoe store.

"Look it over," he said. "Maybe the stuff is no good."

"I can't tell without—"

"All right, there's no charge for trying on."

They were in the store for about half an hour and when they came out, Carol was wearing a pair of Italian sandals and Dan had two shoe boxes under his arm. They started toward the truck and he stopped her and pointed along the arcade. They went a few doors down and turned into a store advertising "Beach and Swim Wear." When they came out to the truck, there was a third package. He helped her in and they drove away.

\* \* \* \*

At the restaurant, they had to wait for a table and they sat in the bar, in a dark corner, drinking slowly. The decor included a lush tropical garden behind glass, behind the bar. Water bubbled over a rocky prominence in the midst of philodendra, banana trees, and dwarf palms. Carol gazed at it long and fixedly. "Have you been to Hawaii?" she asked.

"Never have."

"I was there a couple of years ago. That's the only place I've ever been, except for San Francisco, Los Angeles and Tijuana."

"You were born in San Francisco?"

"Just outside of it, in Richmond. We moved to San Francisco when I was a baby."

"Then you moved to Los Angeles?"

"My sister came down first and I came after high school."

"I always thought a native San Franciscan would throw himself off the bridge before moving to Los Angeles."

"I don't know. The reason I came—there were two reasons—there weren't any good jobs in San Francisco; and everybody said it was warmer in Los Angeles. They were right."

"I guess it's even better in Hawaii."

"It's wonderful in Hawaii. It's just like that." She pointed at the glassed-in garden, "But all over!"

"How is the beach?"

"The beach is—loaded. That's the only thing I didn't like. At Waikiki, you can hardly walk around without sticking your foot in somebody's stomach or face or—something."

"I wouldn't enjoy that."

"No, you wouldn't."

She gazed at the garden with longing. "There must be some place in the world where you can have all that and peace and quiet too."

"I think so," he said, "but you sacrifice comfort and convenience when you go where nobody goes."

"It can be done," she said. "You did it—" Impulsively her hand went to his thigh. "Oh God," she said, "that's awful! Coming from me!"

He patted her hand, comforting her, and her hand became a fist on his thigh, lightly beating.

"Some place," she said, forcing the words through her clenched teeth. "Some place in the world...)

He hadn't managed to reply when the hostess called them to dinner.

* * * *

As they drove northward on the old highway, the surf was on their left, splashing white under an early moon.

"Nice evening," he said, his voice rising over the roar of the truck. "Seems a shame to fold it up so early."

She nodded.

"Like Mexican music?" he asked.

"I like any kind of music."

"We could have a drink at La Cantina and listen to the *mariachis.*"

"All right," she said.

He turned away from the beach at a complex junction, crossed the Freeway approach and drove to a mission village, three or four miles inland. He parked the truck on the street near a small cafe with a lighted streamer reading *La Cantina.* When he helped her down, they could hear the sounds of music played *forte:* guitars, trumpet, and, thinly, violins.

"Very good musicians here," he said. "The food is good, too, if you like Mexican."

She smiled. "Enchilada. Tortilla. Cucaracha."

"Yes," he said, "but this is a clean, well-run place."

"I'm sorry. I seem to have the needle out tonight."

The cafe was in two sections. There were no empty tables in the dining room so they went into the bar. It was small and more crowded than the dining room, what with the six musicians and their instruments, but after a minute, someone got down from the bar itself and there were two vacant stools. They sat down and, after checking with her, he ordered Margaritas.

"Make an exceptionally high class Margarita here," he said.

As if to atone for her earlier remark, she put her hand on his, squeezing. "I'm sure," she said. "I love it. I love the music and I love Margaritas."

*Fortissimo*, the *mariachis* concluded a performance of *Guadalajara.* Carol applauded. The leader, a short, plump guitar player in a purple shirt and tight, gray western pants, approached and asked what they would like to hear. Dan handed the musician two dollar bills.

"They do that *Guadalajara* real well," Carol said.

"They get a lot of practice. Twenty or thirty times a night."

He asked the leader for *Viva Mexico*. The bar was filled to capacity now and the *mariachis* had moved to the curtained alcove between the tavern and the dining room. There were couples at tables along the front and side walls. The rest of the crowd were men, chiefly Mexican workingmen, seated and standing. The street door stood open, but the air was heavy with smoke that hung in blue-gray layers. The room was too small for the music, which thudded and reverberated from the walls and ceiling. The song was spirited, inspirational, and evoked a hearty response. Feet stamped, hands clapped and there were explosive shouts.

Carol's face was flushed as she beat time with her fist on the round edge of the bar and shifted rhythmically from side to side on the stool. She swayed against him, then away and back again, and the liquid in her long-stemmed glass sloshed frostily with the swinging of her arm. The press of the crowd was close at their backs and she hunched forward from it. The standing men, holding cans and bottles of beer, stamped and shouted. In the small room, the throb and din of the music was overpowering.

An unusually burly Mexican in jeans and a denim work shirt lurched heavily against Dan, crowding him into the bar. Dan gave him a hand, grinning.

"*Gracias, señor*," the man said, showing white teeth.

The music stopped. There were shouts, whistles, a flurry of movement around the bar. Someone laughed raucously. Carol was lifting her glass to her mouth when the large man moved unsteadily to set his beer bottle on the bar. He had shifted away from Dan and his arm reached between Carol and her neighbor on the other side. She shrugged away toward Dan, her glass at her lips. Unexpectedly, with no warning, the big *bracero* embraced her grossly.

"Ah—señorita—"

Her face flushed. Her arm slashed down and the bowl of the glass shattered against the bar. She twisted on the stool, her hand gripping the jagged remains.

"No!" Dan said.

With one foot on the floor, he reached to close his left hand on Carol's wrist. His right arm thrust between her and the drunken *bracero*. The bar had fallen silent. Behind it, one of the two bartenders spoke sharply in a low voice.

"*Amigo!*" Dan said sternly. "No."

The big man, his arms enfolding Carol's torso, gazed at him vaguely. Carol's hand opened and she dropped the broken glass. The Mexican was muttering in Spanish, pressing his body against hers. The bartender spoke again, but the big one paid no attention. Carol, hunched on the stool, was cursing under her breath. Dan got both feet on the floor, clutched the belt of the *bracero's* trousers and pushed at his chin with the heel of his hand. The man let go of Carol and stumbled backward on rubber legs, fell against a table, and sat hard on the floor. A woman screamed. The *mariachis* had vanished and were serenading the dining room loudly.

Dan helped Carol off the stool and held her till she was steady on her feet. The bulk of the crowd had pushed back toward the alcove between the bar and dining room, and the few between them and the door scattered to let them pass. He urged her ahead of him toward the street. She was shaking and mumbling. At the threshold, she stumbled and dislodged the sandal on her right foot.

"Goddam it!" she said.

She bent in the doorway and replaced the sandal. Behind them, one bartender had moved into the room and, with the help of some of the patrons, was putting the big *bracero* on his feet. With unnecessary haste, they propelled him toward the street. Carol had straightened and they had cleared the doorway, but not much more, when the big drunk lunged at them from behind. There was a shout. Dan caught most of the weight on his shoulder and shook himself clear. He gave Carol a light push.

"Get in the truck," he said.

She went off and Dan turned in time to meet the *bracero's* charge. A few men had come out of the bar and were trying to talk the drunk into peace, but he was beyond reason. He swung wildly at Dan, who stepped inside the flailing arm to push the Mexican against the plaster wall of the building. A hard fist bruised his cheekbone and when he ducked away, the *bracero's* shoulder thrust convulsively and Dan felt blood well from his nose. He pulled back with his right fist cocked, and then the others were moving in to break it up. Dan went to the curb, blew his nose and cleaned it up as well as he could with his handkerchief.

When he got into the truck, Carol was a long, angular knot against the door. She watched him settle behind the wheel but said nothing. Now and then her lips moved. They were driving through the valley toward the beach when Dan said, "Very unusual. They're mostly nice, gentle people. I don't know where that big one came from."

"He was there," Carol said.

"Did he hurt you?"

After a moment she said, "Not physically."

He looked at her, but said nothing more until he had parked the truck at the dead end and was helping her out. "I'm sorry the evening had a bad ending."

"I'll be all right," she said.

When he took her hand to lead her down over the palisade, she was trembling.

In the house, she excused herself, went outside and was gone a long time. He had his bedroll on the floor and her bed open and turned down when she came back. She had taken off the sweater and had let her hair down around her face. She sat on the bed and looked out the window, her face stiff and hurt-looking. "I'm sorry I was so long," she said. "I was—being sick."

He looked at her across the bedroll. "I regret that it happened," he said, "but since he didn't really hurt you, and it was Friday night, and he worked hard all week for a bare living, so he got a little drunk—maybe you ought not to hold it against him too much."

She said nothing. He went out and when he came back, she was in bed, lying on her back, her eyes blinking in the moonlight. He took off his shoes, socks and trousers and slid into the bag. After a while she said, "Thank you for the shoes and the bathing suit and the dinner and the evening."

"You're welcome," he said. "Have a good rest."

"Do you have to go to work tomorrow?"

"In the morning. If it's a nice day, maybe we can spend part of it on the beach."

"That will be nice."

"It's never crowded on this beach. It's not Waikiki."

"Good," she said.

"Goodnight, Carol."

"Goodnight, Dan."

\* \* \* \*

She woke with a start and he was standing by the bed, dressed in jeans and a sweatshirt, looking down at her. She blinked heavily.

"I'm sorry to wake you," he said.

With a tired, defeated gesture, she rolled the bedclothes back and moved over toward the wall.

"All right," she said.

"I'm going out on the beach for a while. I wanted to let you know."

She lay still, looking up at him. "Oh."

He pulled the covers up over her. "Try and go back to sleep. I didn't mean to disturb you."

He turned abruptly and left the house by the front door.

* * * *

The beach was flooded with moonlight. The surf was quiet, crumbling silver on the sand. Barefoot, he walked the length of the cove to the rocky point where, he had told Carol, the mermaid had sat in the sun. He climbed among the rocks and sat down and looked at the ocean and the moon and now and then at the black, box-like shack against the palisade. At length he walked back across the cove, beyond the shack and in the broad, sunken mouth of the *arroyo*, where it spilled into the beach, he stood a long time looking up toward the Old Man's house. The house itself was not visible from the beach, but he could see the tops of the trees that surrounded it. After a while, he turned from the arroyo and came back to his own beach, where he stood on the wet sand at the water's edge. For several minutes he stood motionless except for the slight shifting of his feet as the surf stirred the sand. Then he stripped, tossing his clothes in a pile on the dry sand, and waded into the sea.

He swam far out and rested a while, his body rolling with the slow swell and returned, swimming with long, leisurely strokes. In the shallow surf, he sprawled, unresisting, to toss and roll with the surge. The tide was shifting and the incoming swells beat at the shore with gradually increasing force. At length, surrendered to it, he let himself be cast up like a chunk of driftwood. He dried himself with his sweatshirt and went back to the house.

He moved quietly. Carol was asleep, but restless.

He heard her murmur a dream-like protest, then turn in the bed. In the kitchen, he dried himself more thoroughly than on the beach, put on fresh shorts and poured himself a glass of milk. He was drinking it when Carol cried out sharply. He went in there and she was in the throes of a nightmare, twisting in the bed and murmuring with suppressed urgency. Then she quieted abruptly, as if the dream had passed, and he had turned away when she cried out—an agonized, muted scream. He returned and she was struggling in a tangle of bedclothes, still half asleep, raising herself on one hand, precariously balanced at the edge. He caught and held her lightly by the arms. She moaned, rousing, sagged against him, then suddenly, fully awake, she tore herself from him and threw herself backward across the bed and crouched, trembling.

"No!" she said. "No—no—don't touch me!"

He stood, uncertain, looking at her. "All right," he said. "I thought you were going to fall off."

"No." She breathed heavily with her head between her arms, her hair over her face. "I'll be all right. Just leave me alone."

"Sure," he said. "Would you like a glass of milk or anything?"

"No—nothing."

"All right. Better cover up. It's cold."

She said nothing and he left her and went to his bedroll and crawled in. After a while, he heard her settle down in the bed and a little later, he fell asleep.

* * * *

In the morning, after he had dressed, he stood at the window for a while, looking alternately at the surf and the sleeping girl. He leaned over, reaching, as if to waken her, then drew back. The sun was up, already reflecting brightly from the water and he drew the curtains over the window, watching her face shadow as the light in the room dimmed. He stood a minute longer, frowning, then moved away and left the house.

At the top of the palisade, a black car bearing the gold insignia of the Sheriff's department was parked on the street across from his truck. Two men in business suits moved along the bougainvillea hedge, pausing frequently to probe under the branches. They were some distance beyond the mouth of the beach path, working back toward it. One of them glanced at him as he topped the cliff and headed for his truck, then returned to his chore.

Dan got in the truck, started it and sat for a minute while the cold engine ground and coughed. The two men in business suits had stopped searching the hedge and were consulting near the path, without apparent reference to the truck. Dan got down, leaving the engine idling, and went to the back of the truck, where he began a methodical inventory of his tools and equipment. He had been at it two or three minutes when the two men approached him. One of them said, "Good morning," and Dan nodded.

"You live down there, on the beach?" one asked.

"Yes," Dan said.

"Alone?"

"That's right."

"You're a gardener?"

"Uh-huh."

"Business license?"

"Up front."

One of them went to the front of the truck and looked into it.

"Do you own the house?" the other one asked.

"No, I rent. From Mister Baumgarten."

The other one returned from the front of the truck. "This shrubbery along here—bougainvillea is it? Somebody's been pruning it, looks like."

"Yes. I pruned it yesterday."

"Is that part of your agreement with Mister Baumgarten? You work out the rent?"

Dan stopped what he was doing and looked first at one, then the other. "I don't mind the questions," he said, "but you're police?"

One of them took out a card and showed it.

"Sheriff," he said.

"Okay," Dan said. "Yes, I take care of Jack Baumgarten's gardening. I also pay rent."

"How long have you lived here?"

"About a year now."

They looked at each other and then off toward the beach. One of them kicked at the rear tire.

"Excuse me," Dan said, moving away. "I'm running myself out of gas."

He walked to the front of the truck, reached through the open window and turned off the ignition. The officers strolled to the middle of the street. One of them smiled. "It's all right," he said. "We're not pushing you."

"Sure," Dan said.

The other one gazed out to sea.

"You'd notice any strangers in the neighborhood, I guess," he said. "This time of year."

"Probably," Dan said. "There aren't many people along here to begin with. Everybody's a stranger."

The officer nodded. "Anybody in the last couple of days?"

Dan scratched his head and shrugged. "One or two. They walk on the beach, come and go. I'm not here through the day." After a minute, he said, "You looking for anybody special?"

They looked at each other, then at him. "A young woman," one said.

"You know her name?" Dan asked.

They shook their heads.

"What does she look like?"

They looked out to sea.

"How bad do you want her?"

"Pretty bad," one of them said.

They walked away to the path and looked down at the beach. Dan returned to the bed of the truck and rattled his equipment. The officers lingered three or four minutes, then turned to their car. Dan waved good-bye and they both nodded. He remained at the truck bed until their car pulled away toward the highway.

In the cab, by way of the rear view mirror, he watched them pause at the boulevard stop. He started the truck and was into a U-turn when they swung into the stream of traffic and headed south, away from town. He turned onto the highway in the other direction and drove some distance to where a break in the center barrier permitted him to turn left and double back toward the Old Man's house. He drove down the long drive, lined with high, naked palms, and pulled up at the gate that led to the patio from the front of the house. He was opening the truck door when the Old Alan came out by the gate. Dan stayed where he was.

"We've got a new type of beachcomber," Dan said. "The Law."

The Old Alan nodded gravely. "They stopped here," he said. "By the way, thanks for pruning the bougainvillea."

"Don't mention it. Is that how those guys work? Just walk along the beach and ask around: 'Did you happen to shoot Freddie Benedict?'"

"They didn't ask me that," the Old Man said.

"All right," Dan said, "what else? In plain clothes? They're not checking out licenses."

"Told me they had a report. A milkman, about four o'clock the other morning, saw a woman stumbling along the highway—south. Along there by the trailer park. Wearing a long dress and no wrap. Appeared to be in trouble. But when the milkman slowed down, she started to run."

Dan waited while the Old Man drew a long breath. "They asked me," he said, "whether I had seen such a person. I said no."

Dan sat back in the seat and brushed at his face with one hand. The Old Man watched him.

"What are you going to do, Dan?" he asked.

"I don't know. Goddam it, I don't know. Listen, if I don't know a thing has happened, it's all right to act as if it never did, isn't it?"

The Old Man looked away. "In a way, I suppose," he said, "you have no choice but to act as if you don't know. But everything that happens has some effect. The people of Hiroshima knew nothing about an atomic bomb. Ignorance is an uncertain guide to conduct."

"Why did you lie to the police?"

The Old Man's face tightened and his eyes drew down at the corners, as if he had come unexpectedly on an atrocity.

"The question is not becoming to you," he said.

"I withdraw it."

The Old Man's mouth moved in a smile. "However, I am an older man and have certain privileges. What is this girl to you?"

"Nothing. A human being."

"Tell me something. If, instead of a young, pretty woman, your guest were a poor, slobbering brute of a person—a bum—a slob? A demented crone, say? What if she were some other sort of human being?"

Dan flushed and his hand moved on the wheel. "That's a dirty, hypothetical question."

The Old Man nodded and stepped back from the truck. "Nevertheless," he said, "I do not withdraw it."

Dan gunned the truck motor and put it in gear. He looked out as if to say a last word, but his lips moved silently and he drove away.

The Old Man watched the truck out of sight, then turned to the gate. In the patio, he moved haltingly, as if by dint of some effort. One of the cats brushed against his leg and he leaned down to stroke it. When the cat left him, he went on and through the rear gate of the patio. He walked by a dirt path to the edge of the cliff and stood blinking in the reflected sunlight. Looking down across the deep cut of the arroyo, he could see the shack from the rear, the small back yard, the kitchen door. While he watched, the door opened and the girl came out, moving quickly but without furtiveness toward the bathroom. She wore only a pair of brief, light-colored panties and her body was white and fragile-looking in the sun. He stayed a moment, then, without waiting for her to reappear, turned and walked back toward the house.

# CHAPTER 5

Dan drove slowly up the narrow hillside street past large, scattered homes on spacious lots. The houses were set far back from the street and the lawns and gardens surrounding them were well established. Each, from its own viewpoint, commanded a vista of both the coastline and the inland canyons and hills. Mailboxes stood at the street in front of the homes, some bearing names and street numbers, others only a number. At one of these, a chain had been stretched across the driveway entrance and a sign read: KEEP OUT—ORDER OF SHERIFF. He slowed the truck to a crawl in passing. There was no sign of activity around the rambling ranch house with the odd, foreign-looking dome on top.

He drove on, turned sharp left and into the drive of an older, less pretentious home. He parked the truck in front of an open garage containing a dusty sport car, stored household goods, and an array of gardening tools. The lot at the rear of the house was a jungle of indiscriminate growth and he sat for a while, looking at it glumly. Then he got down, took a pair of hedge clippers and the long handled pruning shears from the truck bed and waded into the lot. He was trying to separate a giant philodendron from an entangled wild rose when a woman came from the back door of the house and stood watching him.

She was about fifty, dressed in a pair of faded denim slacks, worn bedroom slippers with the toes cut out, and a thin, nylon sweater, spotted with food stains. She was thin, and the bones above her flat breasts showed clearly through the sweater. In one hand she held a glass, half-filled with a clear, white liquid. From time to time, she sipped from it. Her unevenly tanned face showed the ravages of drink and heedless exposure. She shifted her weight frequently, unsteadily.

"Who the hell are you?" she said, staring at his back.

"I'm the gardener, ma'am. My name is Dan."

"Oh yes, I remember. I thought you were supposed to come on Saturdays."

"Yes, Miss Benedict," he said patiently. "This is Saturday."

"It is? Oh yes. Sure it is."

She took a drink from the glass and shifted her weight. Dan reached out to support her, then drew his hand back as she found her balance.

"I'm very sorry about your brother, Miss Benedict," he said.

"Freddie? His name was Freddie."

"Yes, ma'am. Is it all right, what I'm doing here? I thought we could separate these and make two nice plants out of the one."

She nodded. "Very good idea."

He went back to work, his hands careful among the thorny, intertwined branches, and she stayed, watching. As he proceeded, she moved closer little by little, peering over his shoulder.

"You're a very good gardener," she said. "Excellent."

"Thank you, ma'am," he said.

"I recommended you to Missus Carlyle next door. Did she call you? She said she was going to call you."

"Not yet, Miss Benedict. Thanks very much."

He looked over his shoulder and her face hung within inches of his own. She blinked at him and a confused look came over her face.

"Would you care for a drink?" she asked.

"Not right now, thank you."

"There's plenty more, if you want one."

"Thanks just the same, but it's a little early for me."

"Oh," she said.

He moved deeper into the thorny tangle and she straightened up slowly.

"That was one thing about Freddie," she said. "He always had plenty around the house."

He had found the main stalks of the rose and had cleared most of the brittle philodendron and now he began to prune the dead wood.

"Freddie's dead," she said.

"Yes. I'm very sorry."

"Freddie didn't drink."

He said nothing and she moved closer.

"Ouch!" she said.

The cry startled him; he gripped the shears and his face tightened with exasperation. She was pouting at a thorn prick on her left hand; held it out to show him.

"Those rose thorns sometimes fester," he said. "You might like to go in the house and put something on it."

She shook her head and poured some of her drink over her hand. She giggled.

"That'll fix it," she said. "Nothing like vodka for what ails you."

The giggle became a shrill laugh. She lost her balance and he dropped the pruning shears and caught her before she fell into the bush. While he was rescuing her, she lost the rest of her drink, but clung to the glass. He helped her to a rustic bench, where she sat and stared moodily into her empty glass. He started away toward the rosebush and she said, "It's all right. There's plenty more. Freddie locks it up, but I know where the key is." He hesitated, his shoulders hunched, then he went on, but she got up and went after him.

"Come on," she said. "I'll show you where the key is. Be a good joke on Freddie."

"Well, Miss Benedict," he said, "if I'm going to finish this rose-bush—"

"Hell with the rosebush," she said. "Come with me. I want you to know where the key is. Just in case, you know."

When he hung back, she scowled and set her glass down in the grass.

"Do I pay you?" she asked.

"Yes, ma'am."

"Then your time is my time. Come on. I want to show you where the key is."

She tugged at his hand, and then he had to shift suddenly, because instead of going toward her own house, she was leading him away from it along the tight, overgrown steel fence that marked her property line. There was a path, but the ground was uneven and she had difficulty keeping her feet. Several times, he reached out to catch her when she stumbled.

"I didn't realize your property ran to this depth," he said.

She moved one arm in an all-embracing gesture.

"Whole hill," she said. "Benedict Hill. Three gener—three genel—generations."

She was panting with the exertion of the rough walk. She caught the left sleeve of her sweater on a branch and, without pausing to extricate herself, jerked her arm free, tearing a ragged hole in the fabric. The exposed flesh of her arm was blue-white, dry looking.

At the back corner of the lot, a gate opened on an adjoining property. Although the street was hidden by trees and outbuildings, the design and color of the house showed it was the same as that posted by the Sheriff, but there was no sign on the back gate.

Miss Benedict worked the latch and the gate opened quietly. He held it for her, then followed her into a sparsely planted, well-tended back-yard and along a gravel path toward the service entrance. They had not quite reached it when a uniformed officer with a deputy sheriff's arm patch walked into sight from the driveway. Miss Benedict ignored him and went on and the officer confronted her at the back door. Four steps led up to the door and the officer stepped up two of them to face her.

"I'm sorry, ma'am," he said, "the premises are posted. County Sheriff."

She bristled with indignation.

"You must be mad," she said. "This is my brother's house. Family property."

She waved her arm. The officer glanced at Dan, who stood silent, expressionless.

"Kindly step aside," Miss Benedict said.

"I can't," the officer said. "You'll have to get permission from the Sheriff, or a court order."

Miss Benedict looked bewildered and outraged. "I never heard of such a thing," she said. She looked uncertainly at Dan. "Explain to him."

"How long will the place be closed?" Dan asked.

"I don't know," the officer said. "The officer in charge of the investigation will be here around noon. He may release the property at that time. I don't know."

Miss Benedict had begun to shiver, as if with cold. "Listen," she said to the officer, "it's very important to me to go in there. All I want is to show this gentleman where the key is, you understand? You may come, too, if necessary. I'll only be a minute or two." The officer shook his head firmly.

"I'm sorry," he said. "If you want to come back when the investigating officer is here—"

She made a vain effort to achieve a dignified hauteur, then, without warning, attacked the officer violently, kicking at his legs and beating at him with fragile, wiry fists. The officer, taken by surprise, lost his balance and sprawled on the steps. Miss Benedict fell on top of him. By the time Dan moved in to separate them, she had rolled off the steps onto the driveway, where she struggled helplessly for equilibrium. The officer got to his feet, his face flushed and angry.

"Are you responsible for her?" he asked.

Dan started to shake his head, then stopped abruptly, staring at the officer.

"Yeah," he said after a moment. "Right at this time, I guess I am."

"Good," the officer said.

Together they helped Miss Benedict to her feet. She was shaking badly now and her eyes had a pleading look, like those of a dog begging for water.

"Come on now," Dan said, "let's go home. I'll get you a nice drink and you can show me the key the next time."

She made one more attempt to gain poise. Addressing the officer, she said, "This is my gardener. An excellent gardener. Recommend him highly."

The officer brushed at his uniform. "Yes, ma'am." She turned away and permitted Dan to lead her through the gate and along the path to the house. As they approached, a buxom Negro woman in an immaculate white uniform bustled out to meet them.

"Lord, ma'am," she scolded, "you had me scared silly. What you doin', trampin' around this hour of the mornin'?"

In the kitchen, a nearly full bottle of vodka stood on the sinkboard. Miss Benedict broke away from them and seized it. Adroitly, the maid captured the bottle with one hand and reached for a glass with the other. Miss Benedict began to cry.

"Now, now," the maid said, "it's gonna be all right, honey. Fix you a nice, clean glass. You don't want to go drinkin' from the bottle."

Miss Benedict waited while the woman poured a small measure of vodka into a glass and ran water into it from the tap, her nose wrinkling with distaste. Dan waited near the door. Holding the glass out of reach, the maid took her mistress's arm firmly.

"Come along now," she said. "We'll have a nice drink and a nap. Look there now, you tore your sweater…)

They left the kitchen and Dan went back to work. He was pruning the rosebush drastically when the maid came out and stood nearby.

"She settled down all right?" Dan asked.

"Yeah, she'll sleep a while now. I almost had a stroke for sure when I come and find her out of the house. What'd she want—she want to go to Mister Freddie's place?"

"Yes," Dan said. "Something about a key."

The maid snorted. "The key. There ain't any key! Never was. She made that up. Been mumblin' about that key ever since Mister Freddie passed on. She don't need to beg liquor from him. She can buy."

"Maybe it wasn't the liquor so much," Dan said. "Maybe it was his okay she wanted."

"But she's a grown woman. With money. She don't have to ask no-body's say-so."

"I know. But inside, in her own mind, maybe it was his approval she needed, and the stuff about the liquor and the key was just her way of putting it."

The maid shrugged ponderously. "I don't know. Mister Freddie didn't like her drinkin' so much, but he never give her no bad time over it. I know. I worked for both of 'em."

Dan took the pruning shears to the truck, returned with a rake and his square of burlap and began to pick up the cuttings. The maid lingered. "How was Mister Freddie to work for?" he asked.

"Just fine," she said. "Plenty of work, but he leave me alone to do it."

She moved closer and her voice dropped. "Of course, between you and I," she said, "Mister Freddie was what they call—oddball. But that wasn't my business. I done my work and he had his fun. Nobody's business but his own—'ceptin', maybe, for one. The one that shot him."

"Yes," Dan said. "That kind of makes it everybody's business, doesn't it?"

She glanced toward the house, then went on in a conspiratorial tone: "See, Mister Freddie had more of an itch than most men—leastways, he done more scratchin'. He could afford it. I seen the time he had ten different girls in that house—over a week."

Dan shook his head.

"And you know somethin' about them girls? They wasn't normal! I mean, there was somethin' wrong with 'em. In the body, I mean. You know, most men, chasers, they go for them good-lookin', elegant girls, like in the magazines? Mister Freddie—he went for these others—*funny* lookin' girls. Somethin' wrong with their faces, lumpy, or scars like. Or they was crippled some way, in the legs."

Dan raked up the last of the cuttings, picked up the corners of the burlap and carried it to the truck. The maid lumbered at his heels and after he had dumped the load, he leaned against the truck, folding the burlap, and heard her out.

"I like to had fits when I see what went on around Mister Freddie's. Not that he was mean, understand; he was real sweet to them poor girls. But it give a person kind of a crawly feelin' till he get used to it." She shook her head in sad retrospection.

"They were all like that?" Dan asked. "Had some—misfortune?"

"Most, not all. They come and go, you know. One I remember, prettiest girl you ever see. Little blonde girl. Only time I ever scolded Mister Freddie."

He waited, but she seemed deep in reverie.

"You say you scolded Mister Freddie?" he said. "About this girl?"

"She was just a kid, looked like—no more'n eighteen, nineteen years old. I told Mister Freddie, 'Look here, you gonna get in *bad* trouble, foolin' around with them babies.' But he just laughed. 'I wouldn't hurt the girl,' he says. 'Just like to look at her—for contrast.'" She rolled her eyes. "Contrast, he says. Pretty as a picture she was; name was Carol. I remember her name."

From inside the house came a thin, wailing cry. The maid looked around with resignation. "I don't know," she said. "If it wasn't for the good pay—I just don't know."

"Yes," Dan said. "It's quite a lot of responsibility, isn't it?"

"You can say that again."

She turned to the house, massive and plodding, and Dan picked up his tools and put them in the truck.

# CHAPTER 6

When he went into the shack, she was preparing lunch for them, without expertise, doggedly. It was very warm in the house and she was wearing the new bathing suit and had tied her hair in back with a piece of ribbon.

"Was my timing all right?" she asked. "I didn't know when you'd get home. Are you all through for the week?"

"Yes, all through," he said. "Your timing is perfect."

"Mustard or ketchup?"

"Little of both."

"No!"

"Always have both. All-American boy."

"Well, wow-ee!"

He had started out of the kitchen but stopped to look at her.

"You're too young to use an expression like that," he said. "That goes way back."

She was mildly startled. "Oh—I don't know. My sister used to say that. She was older." Her expression softened when she mentioned her sister, then clouded. "My sister is dead."

"I'm sorry," he said, and went out.

When he came back, wearing trunks, she halted in the midst of setting out the lunch.

"Maybe you'd rather make a picnic of it," she said. "Take it down to the beach."

"If you would."

"Well, you said we were going down on the beach."

"It was only a suggestion, not a command. Let's eat first."

They ate at the table in the kitchen.

"Did you see the Old Man today?" she asked.

"For a couple of minutes. Passed the time of day."

Pretty soon she said, "I'm afraid of him."

"Who? The Old Man?"

"Yes."

"Why?"

"I don't know. I just am."

"He's nobody to be afraid of."

"I can't help it."

"Are you afraid of other people? Me, for instance?"

"No, not you."

"Why not? You never saw me till the other day. For all you know, I might be—" He stopped.

She waited and then she said, "Might be what?"

"Nothing," he said.

After a while he said, with gentleness, "It's just that I don't want you to be afraid of the Old Man, or me."

"I'm not afraid of you, but sometimes I'm afraid when I think of the Old Man."

"Then I've got an idea. Let's not call him the Old Man anymore. Let's call him Mister Baumgarten or Jack. You remind me and I'll remind you."

"All right. But maybe it won't make any difference."

"But maybe it will," he said.

"All right."

After lunch, he helped her straighten up the kitchen, and there were some other chores around the house, so that some time passed before they got down to the beach. Aside from a woman with two small children, they had the cove to themselves. The sand was hot in the bright sun, the surf was quiet, the water was very cold. She held tightly to his hand, wading into the surf, and squealed when it swirled around her ankles.

"Is this as warm as it ever gets?" she asked through clenched teeth.

"No," he said, "but this isn't too bad."

"It's too bad for me."

"It takes getting used to."

"Ooh, yes! I bet it does."

"You don't wanna?"

"I don't wanna. Maybe later."

"Okay."

"You go. Go ahead. Swim."

She gave him a push and retreated to the dry sand. He swam out and returned and she winced when the spray from his body whipped hers. "You're a good swimmer," she said. "Who taught you?"

"My father. That is, he taught me how to stay afloat and keep going."

"Did it take a long time?"

"No, not long. One day—I was five years old—my father said, 'Let's go to the beach.' So we drove out to Santa Monica and he showed me a place where the rocks formed kind of a natural pool, when the tide was right. The water wasn't too cold that day, and he said, 'How about going for a swim?' And we went in that pool and fooled around for a while and I don't know exactly how it happened, but before we got out, I knew how to swim."

"Just like that?"

"More or less."

"You and your father made quite a team, huh?"

"He was a good guy."

"Where is he now? Do you see him?"

"He was killed in the war, when I was twelve."

"I'm sorry."

The two children were playing with a red and white beach ball. It got away from them and rolled past Dan toward the surf. He caught and tossed it back to them.

"What about your mother?" Carol asked.

"Well—after the war, she got married again and we moved to Pasadena. Then, after I finished high school, while I was doing the time in the service, they moved back east."

"You never see her?"

"We never had much to say to each other. I don't think she really liked me much."

"That's crazy!"

"Well, she has her life and I have mine."

Carol put her fingertips to her face, then ran her hands over her pale, outstretched thighs.

"I forgot to get suntan lotion," he said. "You'll burn to a crisp out here."

He got to his feet and she reached out impulsively, but too late to catch his hand, so that she caught his knee instead. She let go immediately.

"You can't go all the way to town just to get me suntan lotion," she said.

"Just up to the shack," he said. "I'll make some."

"*Make* some?"

"Only take a minute. It won't smell as fancy as the store-bought kind, but it will work."

She gazed up at him, as if pondering whether to let him go. Then she let him go and, leaning on her hands, she watched him steadily, all the way to the shack and inside, and then continued to stare at the house till he reappeared.

When he came back, he had an oily brown mixture in a fruit jar, a quart bottle of grapefruit juice, and two glasses.

She wrinkled her nose at the concoction, but dipped into it and rubbed it on her legs.

"Feels good," she said, "but it smells awful."

"I know," he said. "You could put some juice in it, give it more tang."

She wrinkled her nose at him, and went on applying the lotion to her legs, arms and shoulders. Finally, she took a deep breath, held it and rubbed the lotion on her face. She let her breath out slowly, looking at him through her fingers. "Not so bad when you get used to it," she said.

"That's my good, brave girl."

She stood up to apply the lotion to the backs of her legs. Her body was supple and firm-fleshed and she showed no niggling shyness over its display. But when he moved to help her with the places she couldn't reach, she went taut and drew away. After a moment, she said, "Please go ahead. I can't reach."

While he rubbed the lotion on her shoulders and back, she stood stiffly with her eyes closed and her hands clenched. The muscles around her shoulder blades were knotty with tension. When he finished, she relaxed gradually, but it was some time before she let herself look at him.

"Thanks," she said. "I guess that guarantees all-over protection."

"It'll help," he said, "but we'd better not stay out too long. Those rays bounce off the water like a bombardment."

They sat side by side, not touching each other. He began moving his legs restlessly and she said, "Why don't you swim if you want to? You don't have to feel stuck here with me."

"I don't feel stuck."

"Yes, but you like to swim, and I like to watch you."

"You're just trying to get rid of me with flattery."

"Yeah. Tell me some more sea stories. Are there boy mermaids or whatever they would be?"

"Mermen? I guess there must be, but who cares?"

"A mermaid might care."

"I never heard any stories about mermen. There's a famous poem about one, but I can't recite it."

"Is it a sad poem?"

"Very sad."

"Then I don't want to hear it."

"That's a lucky thing, because I don't remember it."

"Well, I guess that takes care of the mermaid situation."

"Besides, I was thinking along more practical lines."

"Oh?"

"How about a big, fat lobster for dinner?"

"Mmm, yes."

"All right, here we go."

He started up, was on his haunches, when a masculine shout sounded above and behind them. He froze in the hunched, squatting position. Carol, leaning on her hands, was so rigid that her toes were widely separated and arched backward. Her heart was pounding visibly under the tight bandeau of her swimsuit.

He looked around and upward and there was a man at the edge of the cliff. When Dan looked at him, he gestured frantically. The woman and the two children were at the far end of the cove, clambering over the rocks, paying no attention. The man shouted something unintelligible and Dan got up and walked back toward the palisade. The man was in a business suit and wore glasses that reflected the sun in a concentrated beam. From the foot of the cliff, Dan looked up and the man leaned out and cupped his mouth.

"Hospital!" he yelled. "Where's the nearest hospital?"

Dan pointed south. "Four blocks, turn left."

The man cupped his ear and Dan repeated it in a louder voice. The man nodded and disappeared. Before Dan could turn away, he came back.

"My wife!" he shouted. "Having a baby!"

Dan nodded and waved and the man disappeared again. Dan waited, heard a car start, stall, start again and pull away. He went back to join Carol, who had turned onto her side and was lying with her knees drawn up to her breasts.

"He wanted to know where the hospital was," Dan said. "His wife is having a baby."

She said nothing. She was lying with her back to him and he couldn't see her face. She was so taut that her arched spine showed like pebbles stuffed in a fragile casing. He put his hand on her shoulder and leaned over her and she twisted away, shuddering.

"Excuse me," he said. "I keep forgetting. I'll go get that lobster now."

His feet were in the surf when she called, "Wait, please!"

She ran to him, her stride awkward and uneven in the sand. At the water's edge, she stumbled and he caught her hand. "I want to go too," she panted.

"It'll be pretty cold."

"I don't care. I want to go. *Make* me go."

"Do you know how to swim?"

"A little."

"Float?"

"Yes."

She stood in the surf with her teeth clenched and her hand twisting in his.

"All right," he said. "No hurry. Get your blood used to it, around the ankles. Here—put your wrists in it, like this."

She bent with stiff knees and plunged her wrists into the water.

"Ooh—it's cold!" she said. "My feet are numb."

"Look at it this way," he said. "It's not ice. It's too soft for ice. So you won't freeze."

"Uh-huh," she said. "Sure."

"Ready?"

"No."

"Want to change your mind?"

"No! What's the big rush? Will the lobster go away?"

"Well, I don't have an appointment with him."

She straightened up, looking at her wet hands as if they belonged to someone else. She shook them.

"All right," she said, "let's—go!"

She ran full tilt, with that odd, plunging stride, leaving him flat-footed. When he caught up with her, she was thrashing wildly in waist deep water, moaning and trying to catch her breath. He waited, watching, till she had gained some equilibrium.

"I can't see!" she wailed.

He brushed her wet hair back from her face on both sides, using his fingertips gingerly.

"Oh," she said. *"Now* I see. Go fishing now?"

"More like hunting," he said. "Be sure and let me know if you get too tired."

They struck out toward a jumble of half-sub-merged rocks, where the water foamed, breaking. She swam alongside with a reasonably efficient over-arm stroke. The tide was with them and the surface, though choppy, was not rough. The rocks were about seventy-five yards offshore and there was a mild cross-tide that he was aware of, but she wasn't, so that she kept veering into him, and he would hold the proper course till she bumped him, when, at the first moment of bodily contact, she would kick away from him. Thus he guided her toward the rocks without putting his hands on her. Twice she stopped to rest, peering at him through wet, stringy strands of hair and treading water vigorously. The second time, he advised her, "You're working too hard. Relax. Chest up, head back, breathe deep. Relax. I won't let you drown."

She tried it for a few seconds, until a swell engulfed her unexpectedly, then she thrashed about sputtering. "That's a—great system!"

"When you get the feel of it," he said. "Don't give up. We're almost there."

Approaching the rocks, he swam ahead of her and found a footing, then gave her a hand up, so she could sit on the rock, waist deep in water.

"My God!" she said, panting. "It's ten miles back there."

"No problem," he said. "Wait a few hours till the tide's out. We can walk back."

On the shore, the woman and the two children were watching them. One of the children waved, then the other. Dan waved in response and after a moment Carol did the same, then turned to look out to sea.

"A good mermaid," she said, "could take off from here and just keep going—all the way to Japan, or Singapore."

"Would you rather be a mermaid?"

"I don't know."

"I'm sure it's not all beer and skittles," he said. "Sharks, for instance. Barracuda. The giant squid."

She shivered and drew her knees up out of the water. "You're a regular realist."

"Not always, but now I'm a little hungry and I'd rather have lobster for dinner than hamburger."

He slid into the water. "Don't go away," he said.

She watched his twisting shape sink, turning, till it was a shadow against the rocks, and then she looked here and there, scanning the surface, as if to guess where he would emerge. She missed it by eighty degrees and her head twisted to find him when he came up over her left shoulder some distance away. "Any luck?"

He shook his head, drew breath deeply, and sank again. She crawled over the rocks, and on the sunny side, when she put her face in the water, she could see deep into translucent green. She saw him far down, wriggling, fish-like, his hands groping, pushing at rocks. She was shaking the water out of her eyes when he came up nearby, empty-handed.

"You all right?" he said.

"I'm fine."

He went down again and this time, when she looked under the water, he wasn't visible.

On the seventh dive, he came up with the lobster. He held it up for her and she clapped her hands. It was a big one, with long, weaving antennae. "You feel rested enough to swim home?" he asked.

"Yes. Now?"

"I didn't bring anything to put it in, but I'll let him go if you need help."

"No!" she said, and scrambled off the rock into the water.

Swimming back, they had no problem with a cross-tide, but he had the use of only one arm and the drag of the lobster and they were winded when they hit the beach, where they sprawled in the shallow surf, gasping for breath.

"Why isn't he bright red?" she said. "Is there something wrong with him?"

"No. He hasn't been boiled yet."

She shivered. There were flecks of blood on her left knee. "I did it on the rocks, I guess. I didn't even know it till now."

He splashed water over her knee gently, then reached to brush at it with his fingers. She withdrew it spasmodically, then turned her head away and sat stiffly and he didn't touch her.

"We'd better get him into the pot," he said. "And you've had enough sun for one day."

He got up and she gave him her hand. He released it as soon as she was on her feet and she gathered up her towel and the jar of lotion, the glasses and juice bottle. They crossed the beach and climbed to the shack in silence. She entered by the front door and he went around to the back with the lobster. The box was nearly dry. He dropped the lobster into it and covered it with a piece of plywood.

Inside, the house was hot from the afternoon sun, and he left the back door open. He was at the sink, drawing a kettle of water, when she passed behind him on bare, lightly thudding feet, heading for the shower. Then he was busy for some time over the lobster and his own shower and it was nearly an hour before he saw her again, when he went into the front room.

The curtain had been drawn over the window. She was sitting on the edge of the bed, naked except for a towel drawn over her thighs. In the muted sunlight, her flesh was rosy gold where the swimsuit had exposed her. Her hair was still damp and hung heavily about her face.

He stood in the center of the room and looked at her and she sat quite still, suffering the look, with her face turned toward the dark of the room.

"Listen," she said after a while, "I'm sorry about acting that way— last night in the Mexican place, and today, too, with you. I mean, acting like I would break or something if anybody touched me. I have a thing about it. Ever since I can remember. I don't know why. What I mean is, I don't want you to think it's just you, personally, or anything. It's only that I have this—awful thing!"

"All right," he said, "don't worry about it."

"But you've done all these things for me, and you're a natural, human man, I guess, and I hate being like that with you."

"Well, it's nothing that will drive us to the psychiatric ward."

"Maybe. But there must be something in between—between nothing at all and going crazy."

"I guess so. With time—"

Her small left hand was a tight fist on her thigh. "We can't just sit around and *talk* about it, as if everything could go on forever!" she said. "I don't want to be like that with you."

He said nothing. With a deliberate, premeditated gesture, she pushed the towel aside and got up. She went to him and stood facing him, and after half a minute, she raised her arms and placed her hands flat against his shoulders.

"Help me, please," she said.

Before he would touch her, he waited, forcing her to look at him directly. It took some time, but she opened her eyes and looked at him and he said, "Not as a payment for the food, clothing and shelter?"

"No," she said. "Just for me—and you, if you want to."

He put his hands on her, firmly, but without roughness, and she went rigid. Her shoulder blades were like knives. He held her and made her respond to his kiss before he would stop. He released her then—she was trembling furiously—and she ran from him, but he went after her and when he had his hands on her again, she fought him with panicked savagery. He made a cage of his arms and legs and torso and let her batter and twist and plead herself into exhaustion, but he wouldn't let her go. They were on the bed, then, and she was crying. He held her with one arm and put his other hand on her belly.

"You want to say 'stop' now?" he said.

"It's too late to stop, isn't it?" she said.

"No."

"Yes. It's too late. It's all right. Yes."

After quite a long time, he said, "I'll hurt you a little. I can't help it."

She swallowed—a long, slow undulation in her stretched throat. She was sweating and her face was smudged from the crying. "It's all right," she said again. Then she lunged suddenly and sobbed and said, "Don't be so goddam—*patient* with me!"

"Where did you learn to swear?" he said.

She blinked her drenched eyelids, then, clinging to him fiercely, she began to laugh, on the verge of hysteria. "In the army!" she gasped.

When he hurt her, she made a thin, wiry sound in her throat and stopped laughing. She cried a little from time to time, but not as before.

# CHAPTER 7

They ate the lobster by the open window, watching the sunset. She sat on the bed and he sat on a chair across the table from her.

"So that's what it really tastes like," she said.

"If you say so."

"What shall we do after dinner?" she asked. "After the poor lobster's all gone?"

"Wash the dishes," he said.

"All right." Then she said, "You see how agreeable I can be? You aren't the only one."

"Yeah," he said, "but I don't have to work at it."

"Pretty pleased with yourself, aren't you?" she said. "Smug."

"Not especially. Anybody can catch lobster, if he sets his mind to it."

"Why you dirty!"

She savored the last of the lobster.

"In your opinion," she said, "do women talk too much?"

"By and large. Everybody talks too much. You and I are exceptions."

"Well, I don't want to spoil anything for you, but I have a confession to make."

He was picking up the small litter around his plate with a paper napkin, and his hand clenched on it till his knuckles whitened but he said nothing. After a moment, his hand opened and the tight wad of the napkin fell onto the plate.

"I didn't learn to swear in the army," she said. "I never was in the army."

"That's a relief to me," he said. "It was hard trying to fit you in."

"I picked it up around home. Our parents were very profane, not to say foul-mouthed; also alcoholic. My sister and I were accidents and we cut into their drinking time, so it was pretty tense around home. Our parents did all this cussing, but if we did it, we got slapped or chewed out, or the mouthwash treatment.

"So, when my sister and I were kids—she was eleven and I was about four—we would sneak off by ourselves and practice swearing. We were serious about it, like studying Latin or arithmetic. My sister would say the words, one at a time, and then I would say them. Just the words by themselves. Our parents had a pretty rich vocabulary of their own, and my sister would pick up new ones at school. It was a thrilling, secret game. Later, my sister more or less outgrew it, but with me, I guess it stuck."

He was smiling reflectively.

"And then," she said after a minute, "I'm kind of quick tempered anyway. But if it disgusts you to hear me swear, I'll stop. I promise."

"No," he said, "don't stop." He looked at her for a while. "You were close to your sister, weren't you?"

Her eyes filled and she looked away from him. Her hands were small and helpless on the table.

"She was more of a mother to me. Yes, I was very close to her."

He got up, stacked the dishes and carried them to the kitchen. He was at the sink when she came out, pushing at him with her hip.

"Go away," she said. "Read the paper. Listen to the ball game."

* * * *

When she came in, he was sitting on the chair by the window. The last of the twilight had faded and she saw him as a silhouette. She stood beside the chair and put her hand on his shoulder.

"That was pretty domestic, wasn't it?" she said. "I'm sorry."

He embraced her hips. It was cold in the room and she was wearing only a blouse and panties.

"You'll catch cold," he said.

"It doesn't matter."

"It matters to me."

He turned her to him, pushed her blouse up and kissed her roughly. Momentarily, she shrank, stiffening, then thrust herself at him.

"I forgot for a minute," she said. "I don't have that anymore."

He led her around the table to the bed and covered her. He carried the table to the kitchen and when he returned, she was lying on her back, watching him with eyes like floating opals.

"Sumvitch, how I love you!" she said.

"What?"

He got into bed and began to undress her.

"When I was learning how to swear," she said, "I couldn't pronounce 'son of a bitch.' It came out 'sumvitch.' It took me the longest time."

"It's easy," he said.

"I was only four years old, after all."

"I bet you were a luscious little dish at four."

"No," she said. "I was built like a TV antenna. I was so skinny, I would look at myself in the mirror and cry."

"When you were four?"

"Well, when I was six."

"But you were pretty."

"No, I wasn't even pretty. I didn't get to be pretty till I was about thirteen."

"You came on very strong, once you got started."

"You think I'm pretty?"

"Moderately, yes. And I don't find you awfully scrawny either."

"How do you find me?"

"Like this."

"Yes. Oh! Yes, I'll stop talking now. You talk. Tell me a story—in sign language."

"I don't hear many stories."

"Tell me the old one—the oldest—oldest—please, make me stop talking. Make me…)

* * * *

He was on his elbow beside her, looking out the window and sometimes at her, while she slept. The moon had risen and begun to light the beach. She stirred, stretching her long throat, and mumbled in her sleep. He leaned down, listening, and heard her say, "Time." Suddenly she was panting. "Is it time yet?"

He put his hand on her breast and the panting stopped. She woke, stared up at him vacantly, then smiled and rolled against him.

"What a nightmare," she said. "I was getting dressed—I had to be somewhere in a hurry, and I couldn't find my stockings, and then I didn't know what time it was and I couldn't find my watch. I started screaming for somebody to tell me what time it was."

"It's early," he said.

She was examining him with curiosity and detachment.

"You seem pretty useless," she said. "How come you're not out in the rat race, like other men?"

"Just no good, I guess."

"Lazy," she said. "Good for nothing."

"Uh-huh."

"If you had any ambition, what would it be?"

"An extremely 'iffy' question."

"Never had any ambition at all?"

"No. Desires, hopes, yes. No ambition. I'm a runner."

"A runner?"

"I have a compulsion to escape, run away."

"I don't believe it."

"True."

"You said you were in the service. I bet you never ran away."

"I wasn't in any war. Nothing to run away from. If I had gotten into a war—I don't know. I never was tested."

She reared, indignant; her fist pummeled his chest.

"I'm sorry I brought it up!" she said. "I never met anybody stronger or braver or nicer or—anything than you."

"You're a sweet kid. Kiss me."

"Now cut that out. I'm serious."

"So am I. I just gave you a perfect example of me running away. I tried to duck the discussion."

"I'm talking about big, important things."

"All right, but it's the same pattern."

"Tell me something—one important thing—you ran away from?"

"That marriage for one."

"Ho, ho. You mean it was all your fault?"

"That's not the point. Whose fault it was doesn't matter. The point is, there was an undertaking I had signed up for and when it got rough, I backed away from it. Maybe I could have worked it out with her, if I had tried."

"Did she try?"

"That doesn't make any difference."

"Listen, marriages break up all the time!"

"Yes, but many don't break up. You want to assume that the only ones that last are the easy, happy ones?"

"No, but—"

"That's all I'm saying. Some people try harder. Some people hang in and work it out. Some people run away."

"All right! You stubborn son of a bitch—the ones that stick it out, even when they're miserable—they're masochists!"

"That's a rationalization."

"It's not either. Any psychiatrist—"

"Okay. It's a psychiatrist's rationalization."

This time, he caught and held her and pulled her on top of him and, after a minute, she stopped struggling and lay with her head on his shoulder.

"How did we get into this intellectual foolishness?" he said.

She put her face against his neck and kissed him and he shivered.

"All right," she said, "but you're not a coward."

"I never said I was, but probably I am."

"Then so is everybody."

"That would be some comfort, but it's not true."

"I give up," she said. "You're a bum."

"Yeah."

"A slob."

"No, not a slob."

"You're a lousy slob of a beach bum."

"Okay. I make a good mattress, though, huh?"

"No. Too lumpy."

She got up and he held her by the wrist.

"Where do you think you're going?"

"Leggo," she said. "I have to."

"Better put something on."

Dressing herself, she moved heavily in the dark, stamping her feet.

"You're not only a bum and a slob," she said, "you're a fussbudget!"

"I know. That's another compulsion I forgot to mention. Bossiness. Would you like a drink?"

"Not till I get back," she said.

She went away and he got up, put on his trunks and a sweatshirt and lighted a lamp in the kitchen. He held the whisky bottle up to the light and there were two good drinks left in it. He made them on the shelf and handed her one when she came in. She drank in sips, holding the glass in both hands, turning and stroking it. He was standing with his hips against the shelf and she stood close, facing him, and leaned into him with her pelvis, her back arched.

She sipped from her glass and looked up at his face, her eyes moving with method and concentration, as if she were analyzing his face, preparing to paint or photograph it. After a while, she held the glass up between them and peered at him through the amber liquid. He made a grotesque face at her and she smiled, but to herself, secretly. They drank in silence, until she said, "You didn't believe me, did you, when I said I went to the nudist camp?"

"Yes, I believed you."

"I had a good tan in those days. It's hard for me to get a tan, with my complexion."

"Did you like being a nudist?"

"Well, yes and no. The nude part of it was all right, once I got used to it. I got over being so damn self-conscious. But nudists—the ones I met—are a bunch of nuts. They're hipped on something, like diet, or politics, or astrology or some goddam thing and that's all they ever talk about—day in and day out."

"You're just too normal."

"Yes. Look at me. Just a few hours ago, I wasn't normal at all. Now I'm normal."

She studied him and her glass. "I only went to the nudist camp in the first place because of my sister. Whatever my sister wanted was all right with me. I would never have gone nudist on my own. But I think I know why my sister wanted to do it."

He said nothing, but waited, and she set her glass down on the shelf and put her arms around him and her face against his chest. Her hands clenched at his back and when she spoke, her voice was absorbed by his woolen shirt and had a muffled tone.

"My sister," she said, "was beautiful—from the neck down. A man would say she was stacked, you know? Now, in ordinary life, the main thing a girl has, that shows, is a face. But my sister didn't have a face—because of an accident. Before, she was quite pretty, but after the accident, nothing—worse than nothing. She was twenty-four then."

Her fingers twisted at his shirt and she rubbed her face against his chest.

"If she'd been born that way," she said, "if she'd had time to learn to live with it—but this way, it was like dying."

"Yes," he said.

"So anyway, I think the reason she wanted to go to the nudist camp was to get a more even break. You know what I mean? Not that a nudist camp is much of a hunting ground. It's not even especially sexy. If it was, it would be closed down. You don't go to a nudist camp to show off how you're stacked. My sister knew this all right, but she had to do something to take the curse off that poor, horrible face. She had to prove to somebody she wasn't like that all over!"

She shifted her feet, turning, and picked up her glass. She leaned against him with her hip and shoulder, as against a post or wall.

"You told me your sister was dead," he said. "Did she die in an accident?"

She said nothing. It was as if she hadn't heard him. She finished her drink at her accustomed pace and set the glass down. "Yes and no," she said. "Do you think—could we go for a walk on the beach?"

"If that's what you'd like to do."

"Yes, that's what I'd like to do right now."

They went into the living room and she would have gone on outside, but he caught her at the door. "Oh—you!" she said.

She was wearing one of the new skirts and a blouse and nothing else. He took down the woolen shirt he had given her the first day and made her put it on.

"If you had any sense," he said, "we wouldn't have to go through this every time."

She stamped her bare feet and went out, as if to run away, but she was waiting where the steps ended and the steep path began, and she took his hand for the descent. They walked near the water, south toward "mermaid point." There was a strong breeze, it had grown cold and the surf was rough and noisy. They didn't try to talk, but walked with long strides, their faces turned from the surf spray. When they reached the rocks, she was panting and they had to run up the beach into the lee of the rocks when the surf chased them. But as it retreated, she tugged at his hand.

"Come on!" she shouted. "Let's keep going."

He held back, studying the surf, and she let go of him and ran on toward the water again and around the point. The surf boiled white among the rocks which lay in a tumble at the base of the high boulder that marked the point. She was making her way over the low rocks, plunging and heedless, when he caught up with her. Before he could reach her, she slipped and crouched, clinging, one leg outstretched, with her foot in the water between two rocks. He lifted and righted her and held her with one arm and they jumped clear of an approaching breaker into the next cove. She turned her back to the spray and laughed into his shirt.

"It's coming in, I guess," he said.

She had started on and she looked back at him. "What?" she called.

He gestured toward the water and she turned away and went on ahead of him. The cove was long and shallow, littered with cast-up debris. The palisades rose on their left. At the far end of the cove, the cliff plunged sheer to the water, with no jumble of rocks at its base. That would be as far as they could go by land.

They had nearly reached the far limit of the beach when she broke into a run, that awkward plunge, more awkward than usual over the littered sand. He quickened his pace, but she reached the cliff before him and turned, braced against it, breathless and laughing. Then she crumpled, sliding downward against the rock wall. He caught her, but lost his balance and fell with her and they lay in a heap on the sand. The surf was thunderous and imminent. She put her hands on his face, drew him down and kissed him. Their mouths were stiff with salt. She was saying something, but the sound was lost in the roar of the surf. He put his ear to her mouth.

"…end of the line."

"What?"

She twisted under him and reached out with one hand to stroke the rock wall.

"All I said was," she shouted, "so this is the end of the line."

He shook his head sternly, gathered and lifted her, rising to his feet. She put her arms around his neck and clung to him with her face at his throat. The tide was high on the beach and he had to walk close to the palisades.

"Where are we going?" she said.

"Home," he said. "But I doubt if we can make it on foot."

She turned in his arms, looking along the beach in the direction he was taking her. The surf broke high on the point, foaming among the low rocks as it retreated, then returning to shatter against the cliff. She tightened her arms around him, shivering.

He turned toward the surf, put her on her feet and held her in both arms with her back against him, getting his breath.

"Now what?" she said. "We jump from rock to rock?"

"Too rough. Can't stay on your feet in that stuff." She looked toward the nearly submerged point. The shack was not visible from where they stood.

"All right," he said, "come on." He moved in front of her and crouched. "Get on."

"What?"

"Piggyback."

"You're crazy!"

"Only way," he said. "Climb on and hold tight." After a moment, she pulled her damp skirt up around her hips and mounted his back gingerly.

"Higher," he said, "and keep your head up."

He shrugged her upward, found her dangling feet and crossed them over his belly. She locked her ankles and clung to his shoulders. He started into the water, bearing toward the point, but on a wide arc, heading seaward around it. He waded carefully, as if his feet had to feel out each step, and hunched forward to counteract the drag of her weight against the tide. She rode high on his back with her long neck stretched and her face tilted against the spray. He lost his balance in the wash of the first breaker, went down on one knee, so that she was immersed to the shoulders. She tightened the grip of her legs and arms, but made no sound, and he got up in time to meet the next one properly. He was able to wade far enough out to clear the main jut of the point, then he had to swim.

It was possible to swim with the girl on his back only because the breakers, though heavy, were evenly spaced and the waves were not high. He swam with a powerful breast stroke, keeping his shoulders well up so the girl would not be subjected to the full impact of the breakers. His progress was slow, but adequate to take them to a point from which he could avoid the rocks and return to his own beach.

The return was more strenuous than the outward trip. With the weight on his back, he couldn't ride the surf properly, but swam on a long, obtuse angle across the swells, on a bearing which, if maintained, would carry them far beyond a convenient landing point. He was badly winded and had to fight his own helplessness in the surging troughs between waves. One broke unexpectedly over them and he lunged upward to keep the girl's face clear, then nearly foundered when they slid down into the trough. They were far enough out that he could rest through three or four waves before tackling the breakers again. The girl's mouth worked at his ear.

"You'll kill yourself," she said. "Let me get off."

"Just hang on!" he panted.

He swam with the next wave, which carried them well in, and from there on, they would be in the surf. He was panting heavily and he twisted in the water, looking back, looking for the white crest of the next wave. It rose close behind them and he drove up into it as it curled and swam desperately to get on top of it. Then it broke and they plunged with it, and all he had to do then was to stay on his belly and keep the girl upright and not be in a hurry, because the breaker was in all the hurry he could use.

They were lucky. It was a long one and by the time it died under them, he had found the bottom with his feet. He had to swim again as the backwash swept them seaward, and the next breaker hit them before he could get away, but it was largely spent. When it struck, he loosened the girl's ankles and shook her off his back, but held firmly to her wrist and he was on his feet, hauling her up into his arms before it could tumble her in the bruising gravel. Carrying her up on the beach, he staggered and when they were beyond reach of the surf, he collapsed with the girl under him, but fell on his hands with his arms locked and rolled away in time. She rolled against him. She was trembling all over and her fist gouged at his throat.

"You," she gasped, "you—beautiful—son of a bitch—you."

\* \* \* \*

Much later, after they reached the shack, he was still fighting for breath. In the kitchen, he lit the oven and she stood, humbly quiescent, while he stripped off her clothes. There was sand on her face and legs and arms and her wet hair clung to her face and neck. She gave him a look of sly penitence from under her eyelids.

"You going to spank me now?" she said.

He was stripping himself.

"It's a temptation," he said.

He opened a beach towel and wrapped it around her.

"You bought me new clothes," she said, "and I got them all wet."

"They'll dry."

"If it was the other way around," she said, "I'd feel like beating the hell out of you."

"You want somebody to beat the hell out of you?"

She looked at him quickly and looked away. "I don't know."

He put his arm around her. "Come on," he said. "To the shower."

# CHAPTER 8

He was asleep with the girl beside him; but she was not sleeping. She crouched on her knees, forming a low mound, with her face turned to the window. The window was closed, but the throb of the surf was heavy in the room. The moon hung low over the water and made a broad yellow path to the beach.

The girl's face dropped till her forehead rested on her hands on the narrow sill of the window. She made a sound in her throat, of pain, not passion. After a while, she turned, leaning on her hand and looked down at him. "Dan," she said.

He woke quietly and his arms reached for her, but she evaded them. "What?" he said.

He ran his hands through his hair, raised himself on his elbow and waited. She moved away on her knees, as if to escape.

"Oh God," she said.

"What is it, Carol?"

"Listen," she said, "I'm afraid here. I can't stay here any longer."

"Where do you want to go?"

"I don't know. Somewhere...)

She was shivering, so he drew her into the bed and covered her. He was on his elbow and she lay stretched taut along his body. Looking up, she could see his pulse in the arched column of his neck.

"I'll have to make some arrangements," he said.

She said nothing. Even in the warm bed, she continued to tremble and he put his hand on the small of her back, stroking.

"Go to sleep," he said. "Try not to be afraid."

Her trembling diminished gradually. After a long time, she turned on her side, facing him. She put her mouth on his chest, and he held her with one arm, leaning stolidly, waiting for her to sleep.

At daybreak, he drew the curtain over the window, got up and dressed in trunks and a sweatshirt, and took the strongbox down from the shelf in the wardrobe. He inspected its contents briefly and took from it a bank passbook in a plastic holder. He looked at the girl to make sure she was asleep, then left the house.

* * * *

The Old Man, wearing slippers, a long, embroidered dressing gown and a scarf, was drinking coffee and reading. In the tentative morning light, the old Spanish room was a monotone.

"I'll get you some coffee," the Old Man said.

The two cats roused, blinking, and stalked about on a long sofa. The Old Man brought the coffee. It was steaming and Dan sipped at it with caution. They sat in silence while the cats cleaned themselves and, at length, first one then the other, left the sofa and the room.

"Something has come up," Dan said. "A crisis. I guess it can't wait till tomorrow."

"In the nature of a crisis," the Old Man said.

"You told me once, you keep some cash around the house."

"Yes." After a moment he said, "How much do you need?"

Dan weighed the passbook on his palm. "In the Federal Savings, I have about five thousand. They'll give it to you on my written authorization."

The Old Man showed some surprise.

"I don't know why I didn't mention this before," Dan said. "It didn't mean a thing unless I told you. But some time ago, I talked to them down there and made an arrangement that they would let you withdraw the money on my signature. So I know they will."

"Oh," the Old Man said. "I wasn't thinking whether they would or not. Why would you make such an arrangement?"

Dan shrugged.

"I was living on your property, alone. I didn't have anybody closer than you. It was a form of insurance, but better than insurance. If something happened to me, you might have a mess on your hands. The least I could do—see you had no expense."

The Old Man cleared his throat slightly and looked away.

"I see," he said. "Excuse me."

He left the room and returned with a sheaf of currency in one hand and a memo pad and ballpoint pen in the other. He handed Dan the money, but hesitated over the pen and paper.

"Look," he said, "inasmuch as I don't have a mess on my hands, no reason to go through this ceremony. You're welcome—"

Dan shook his head.

"I won't take it that way," he said, "as loan or gift. I may be back, I may not."

Reluctantly, the Old Man released the pad and pen. He watched as Dan wrote; the seams of his face deepened. When Dan returned them, he put the pen in a pocket and walked about the room, slapping the memo pad on his palm.

"I know better than to ask questions," he said, "but you ought not to put too much strain on me, at my age.

"Well, I don't know," Dan said. "The most comfortable way I can put it—we decided to go fishing."

"Mexico?"

"I guess so."

The Old Man glanced at the memo pad. "I don't begrudge it, understand," he said, "but have the rates gone up so much? You plan an extended trip?"

"I can't say. It may be—and then again...)

The Old Man sat down.

"Dan," he said, and halted.

"Maybe this will help," Dan said. "When I was about seven years old, I got lost once, in the mountains up around La Canada. We were having a family picnic and I took off on a private hike. I didn't get found till after midnight, half frozen and scared crazy. I mean, it took me a week to get over being scared.

"My father talked to me. He didn't chew me out for running off and making trouble. He just pointed out that most of those people, tramping around the mountains in the cold, didn't have to be there. Aside from the paid officers, they could have been home with their feet in the fire. Because who was I to them? But there they were, out looking for me. And he said—I can hear him say it—'Those people were out there because they felt a responsibility; not just for one dumb kid, but for the human race.' And then he said there were a lot of different ways to get lost; you could get lost without ever leaving home.

"Well, the way I say it now, it sounds, you know, like do-goodism. But I never can forget it. And there was another thing he said, but I can't remember whether it was at that time or later. He said there aren't any laws covering a person's responsibility to the human race; in fact, most countries have laws against it. And so, he said, that more or less leaves it up to you—meaning me. And that's about the longest speech I ever made in my life. Excuse me."

The Old Man looked at him across the old room. It was day now, but without sun, and the contrasts between light and shadow were sharper.

"As simple as that?" he said.

"Just about."

"A good man, your father," the Old Man said. "Of course, you were both younger at that time."

"True."

Dan got up. He made a tight roll of the currency and held it in one fist.

"Thanks for everything," he said. "I'll put my equipment and stuff in the house. If I don't come back when the rent runs out, do what you want with it."

The Old Man brushed at his face.

"All right," he said. "*Vaya con dios,* Dan."

"Goodbye," Dan said, "Take good care of the cats."

When he went into the shack, the girl was asleep. He made coffee and poured juice for two. He drank a cup of coffee and the juice, standing, then went outside and climbed the palisade to the street.

The truck bed was a lumpy, canvas-covered mound, soggy with morning damp. He pulled the canvas off and laid it flat on the street. There were two power mowers and one hand-operated edger and he carried them on his back, one at a time, down over the cliff to the shack, where he set them in the backyard. He brought the heavier items first and when he came down with the edger, the girl was watching him through the kitchen window. He waved and she smiled faintly and raised a cup of coffee as an offering. She was wearing the leather jacket over a pair of panties and she hadn't combed her hair. Among its snarled strands, her face was drawn and sick looking.

"How can I help you?" she asked.

"Well," he said, "how are you at sprucing up old fishing tackle?"

"I'm quite good. Is that where we're going, fishing?"

"Why not?" he said.

"All right, where is it?"

"I was kidding. I started the bathroom heater. Why don't you take a leisurely shower and relax?"

"No, I want to do something." She put one hand to her hair, then her face. "Oh," she said. "I'm a mess, huh?" She looked down at the leather jacket and closed it where it had gaped over her belly. "Excuse me," she said. "I must look like a real bag."

"No," he said, "but you look—unwell."

"Yeah. Incidentally, do you have any aspirin?"

"I think so."

He searched a cupboard and found a small, flat tin of aspirin.

"Where do you hurt?" he said.

The corners of her mouth twitched.

"None of your business," she said.

"You ought to eat something besides coffee."

"Please," she said, "don't make me any sicker than I am.

"I'll buy you a good breakfast down the road."

"Which way are we going, down the road?"

He finished his coffee and put the cup down.

"South," he said.

She said nothing, but watched him leave the house and climb to the street.

The next time he saw her, she was dressed in skirt, blouse and sandals, and had combed and tied her hair and applied powder and lipstick. By then, he had emptied the truck and was storing the smaller implements in the front room.

"Feel better?" he asked.

"I don't know," she said. "Why don't you feel me and find out?"

"You feel better," he said. "I can tell."

*"Now* let me help you?"

"Okay."

He got down a somewhat battered suitcase and opened it on the bed.

"Just fill it up," he said.

When he got the bedroll out, she said, "We going to camp out?"

He laughed at the alarm in her voice. "Only in an emergency," he said. "It looks better this way. Can't go fishing without a bedroll."

"Oh. Naturally."

She had the suitcase ready by the time he had brought in the heavy equipment. He made three trips up over the cliff. There were two fishing rods and he took one apart, but let the second one extend past the end of the truck. He covered the suitcase and bedroll and the rest of the tackle with the canvas and tied it down. The morning fog was clearing, there was hazy sunshine, but the canvas was still soggy.

The girl was waiting at the shack with her sweater over her shoulders. He turned off the gasoline heater and stove and he drained the stove and put the gasoline in a metal can outside the shack. He made a quick survey of the wardrobe and the cupboards and made sure the front door was locked.

"Should you tell the Old—Mister Baumgarten you're going away?" she asked.

"I did," he said.

"Oh."

"I told him we were going fishing."

"What did he think about it?"

"I don't know. He didn't say."

"You didn't ask him?"

"No. But it was necessary to see him, because it was Sunday and the banks are closed, and I had to get some money."

As he helped her up the cliff toward the truck, he said, "You mustn't be afraid of the Old Man."

"All right," she said.

When they were in the truck, he said, "I have to make one stop."

He drove back toward the town, turned into a small shopping center and pulled up in front of a drugstore, just opening for the day.

"There must be some items we need from the drugstore," he said. "Citronella for one, and whatever you want."

She blinked at him.

"What I have to do," he said, "is to see a guy about taking care of my customers. We can save some time if you'll do the shopping while I see him."

She looked at the store and at him again. "All right. Citronella?"

"Yes."

He got down and helped her out. She lingered near the truck as he got back in and started away. Not till he had disappeared did she turn and move toward the store. Entering, she paused to look back in the direction he had gone.

He drove into the town and stopped at a large house set back from the street. A sign in a front window read: "A. Lemoyne—Landscape Gardening." There was no sign of life and he stood at the door a long time before it opened. Then he went in and remained about ten minutes. When he came out, a man in blue jeans came with him and watched him off.

He drove to the drugstore, went inside and the girl wasn't there. He searched carefully and left the store without asking any questions. He showed no sign of agitation except for a rhythmic flexing of his left first. He glanced around the shopping center and she was not in sight. None of the other stores was open and there was no place she could be hidden.

He got in the truck and sat for a couple of minutes, drumming with his fingers on the wheel. There was a fringe of sweat on his upper lip and he wiped it away with the back of his hand. He started the truck, drove to the highway and, after a moment's hesitation, turned south. In the short time since they had left the shack, the Sunday traffic had thickened to a steady stream in the faster lane. He drove slowly along the outer edge of the road, looking for her.

A cluster of people stood at a bus stop on the northbound side of the highway, but she was not among them. He passed the trailer park and then the long, high plain where the Old Man's house sat, far back among the palms. At the Old Man's drive, he hesitated, then went on along the highway. There was a slow curve where the road dipped, crossing the arroyo, and beyond, from his position, the street was hidden. He had made the first segment of the curve and was pushing the truck for the climb ahead, when he caught sight of her.

She was walking well off the road, on the right side, not hurrying. In one hand she carried her beaded bag, in the other a paper sack. She was looking straight ahead and she didn't look around when he slowed the truck beside her. Even after he had pulled off the road and come to a full stop, it was a long moment before she took notice of him. Then she stopped and he got down and walked around the truck to meet her on the off-street side.

"You wander around this part of town," he said, "you get lost. You lose things."

She said nothing. He opened the door and helped her into the seat. When he got in beside her, she was sitting with her back straight and her hands folded over the purse and the paper sack in her lap. He drove half a mile before she spoke. Then she said, in a clear, round voice, "There was a chance you were ditching me. I didn't feel like hanging around a goddam drugstore."

"Well," he said, "I guess I wouldn't either. But if we're going fishing together, you've got to have more faith."

With an abrupt gesture, she thrust the paper sack across the seat.

"Citronella," she said. "What's it for?"

He looked at her. "Mosquitoes," he said.

"Oh," she said thoughtfully.

"Oh what?"

"The guy in the drugstore, when he got it for me, he kind of leered. I thought maybe it was an item you should be buying, not me."

"Well," he said, "when your faith starts to go, it goes all to hell, doesn't it?"

She moved across the seat and put her face against his arm. He looked at her and saw she had been crying.

"You'll be all right," he said. "You need some breakfast."

Her fingers twisted at his shirtsleeve. They were leaving the last of the beach community by way of a long curve seaward. Looking back, over her head, he could see the jut of his own point and beyond it, receding, the tops of the palm trees around the Old Man's house. Then on the next curve, the land fell, and the point and the Old Man's trees passed from sight.

# CHAPTER 9

They drove down the narrow spit of land that connects Coronado with the southernmost section of American California and is called "The Silver Strand." It was midday and the sunlight was dazzling on the water on both sides of them.

"Is that Mexico?" she asked.

Ahead, a blue-toned promontory thrust south and west.

"Somewhere along there, yes," he said. "We'll have lunch in Tijuana."

Approaching the border, the broad highway was progressively narrowed by a series of artificial barriers, so that traffic was funneled in a single lane through the Mexican port of entry. Officers of the California Highway Patrol directed traffic, which piled up for several blocks before the checkpoint.

Carol sat tensely by the window, looking out as they inched forward. Bright spots of color burned in her cheeks. An officer waved them forward and she turned her face from him with a show of casualness.

"Boy," she said, "if you were trying to duck out of the country, you could get pretty nervous along here."

"I guess so," he said. "If they know what they're looking for, they don't miss much."

"What's that shack over there, where they're lined up on the sidewalk? They look like mostly kids."

"Mostly. They try to check out the teenagers."

"On account of dope?"

"More or less."

"Do the Mexicans check too?"

"Not to the same extent. You're welcome to enter and spend your money."

"How about the citronella?"

"Watch it," he said. "Your faith is slipping."

She put her hand on his thigh, squeezing. "Not really."

The line moved ahead and he pulled into the narrow dock of the port of entry. A Mexican officer in a blue uniform leaned into the truck.

"Where are you going in Mexico, señor?"

"Ensenada."

"Fishing?"

"Yes."

The officer glanced toward the back of the truck. "You bring provisions, señor? Food, liquor?"

"No, sir."

"Okay. Good fishing, señor."

"Gracias."

The truck rolled slowly from the dock, past the unkempt border station, toward the arching, narrow bridge leading into Tijuana. Carol settled in the seat, put her head back and closed her eyes. She was breathing heavily and the two discs of color in her face were bright for a few moments, then slowly faded.

On the winding coast route of Baja California, there was more returning traffic than southbound and he drove slowly, wary of the poorly engineered twists and turns. A station wagon with a California license, loaded with fishing and camping gear, swung wide on an approaching curve, and Dan brought the truck to a stop on the edge of the road. Carol, looking down over the cliff, shivered.

"Some drop, huh?"

"Roads cost money," he said.

The station wagon passed and they went on.

"Looks as if we'll have plenty of room in Ensenada," he said. "Everybody's going home."

"Is it much farther?"

"Not far now."

* * * *

They drove through the dusty town. The harbor, on their right, was crowded with ships.

"Look at the boats!" she said. "From everywhere in the world. Like San Francisco."

"It's a major port," Dan said.

"I didn't know."

He pulled off on the shoulder of the road, south of the main part of town.

"There's a good motel, with a restaurant, a couple of miles down the road," he said. "I thought we might stay there, while we look for something more permanent."

"Permanent?"

"It's up to you. 'Permanent' means like a week or longer."

"Oh. The motel sounds fine."

He got back on the road and drove south. She had been riding with her hand on his thigh, but now she sat by the window, not touching him, her face closed. At the motel, she waited in the truck while he arranged for the room and got the suitcase from the back of the truck, and she said nothing as they climbed to the upper tier of rooms, following the Mexican boy with the suitcase. When they went inside, she stood apart while Dan tipped the boy and ordered a bottle of whisky and ice.

The room was clean and tastefully furnished, with twin beds. Large windows opened on a balcony overlooking a swimming pool. Carol excused herself and went into the bathroom. When she came out, the whisky and ice had been delivered and Dan was on the balcony, looking down at the pool. She sat on one of the beds with her hands in her lap. Dan came from the balcony and made drinks for them.

"Salud."

She raised her glass, but wouldn't look at him. She drank in that spasmodic way she had done the first time, at the beach shack, holding the glass in both hands, her fingers restless. Each swallow was a separate, sustained effort.

"Cheer up," Dan said after a while. "No sharks in the swimming pool."

She gazed at him. "I feel like I did a horrible thing to you."

"You do?"

"Like you were a flower and I tore you up by the roots."

"A flower! What kind of a flower?"

"All right, not a flower—a tree, maybe."

"You flatter yourself. You're not big enough to tear me up by the roots."

"Oh, you're so damn—realistic!"

"You just don't know me yet."

"Won't you even let me feel sorry about tearing you up—making you lug me all the way to Mexico?"

"Sure," he said. "Here, have another drink and feel twice as sorry."

He made two more drinks. "Salud."

She hesitated, then raised her glass.

"All right, goddam it—salud!" she said.

He grinned at her. "I don't mean to snarl at you. You seemed moody. Not good for you. Depression is a self-indulgence." He looked into his drink, frowning.

"What's the matter?" she said. "That sounds very wise to me. 'Depression is a self-indulgence.'"

She was watching him now.

"I heard it somewhere," he said.

"From the Old Man?"

"Jack Baumgarten, yes."

They were looking at each other over their glasses, sitting across from each other on the separate beds. "What the hell are we talking about?" he said.

"I don't know."

He set his glass on the table between the beds and she did the same, watching him steadily. He leaned across the space between them and she moved over him without urging, self-propelled, her hands searching his face, as if she were blind and were trying to identify him.

"Little Carol," he said.

"Big Dan—oh, big, big, big Dan!"

* * * *

They drove over the empty plains to Estero Beach, six miles south of the town. The motel and trailer park were filled and children were playing everywhere. There were many fishermen coming and going and a good many small boats.

"Lots of people," Dan said.

"Yes," Carol said. "Too many people."

"Lunch?"

"Yes, lunch."

After lunch, they drove back to town and loitered by the harbor, then went along the coast at the north end of town, where there were "for rent" signs on occasional seaside houses. In a real estate office, they found a Mexican woman who showed them pictures of several available houses.

"Señor—señora," the woman said after a while, "I think I have something you will like. You have transportation?"

"Yes," Dan said. "Do you mind riding in the truck?"

"No, señor."

The three of them got in the truck and the woman showed them where to go. The house was of concrete blocks, square and uninspired in design, but cool inside, and clean. It sat by itself on the brow of the beach slope and there were no other houses in sight. From a point between the low and high tide lines, they could see a part of the harbor, three quarters of a mile southward. The woman who was showing them the house said she could get them a maid for ten dollars a week.

"There are only the two of us," Dan said. "I don't think we'll need a maid. How much is the rent?"

"Twenty-five dollars a week, señor."

"Very good," Dan said.

He gave her fifty dollars for two weeks' rent and the woman wrote him a receipt in English. They took her back to her office and drove into town for supplies.

* * * *

The weather was hot and dry and in the town it was dusty and the smells were high and pervasive, but the house was upwind from town, surrounded by chaparral and manzanita and a few pepper trees, and there was a sea breeze. Dan brought the things in from the truck and they undressed and went down on the beach. The water was very cold and Carol declined to go swimming. When Dan came out of the water, she got up and dried him with a large beach towel.

"You're getting to be quite a woman," he said.

"I got quite a man."

"What have we got for dinner?"

"Not much. I didn't buy any meat. I was afraid to. It looked funny."

"Well, since you're so nice to me, I'll get a few fish."

"Just like that, huh?"

"Why not? You don't believe it?"

"Yes—that's the trouble. If you say it, I believe it."

"That's the way it should be."

She threw the towel at him and ran to the house. They returned with the two fish poles and a can of bait. He cast both lines into the surf and anchored the butt ends of the poles in the sand.

"Now what?" she said.

"Patience."

She stood with her back against him, leaning.

"I know if you say so," she said, "you'll catch fish. But what if—just in case?"

"I guess we'd have to go to bed hungry."

"You could get a lobster maybe."

"Not right now," he said. "The water's murky to begin with and the light is wrong. I can't see much down there."

A large freighter moved seaward from the harbor, bearing north. She was black against the low sun and the colors of her flag were obscured. They watched in silence till the ship was a distant mound, high on the horizon.

"Did you ever think," she said, "about getting on one of those and going someplace—some other country, and just never coming back?"

"Sure," he said. "I thought of it at the time of the divorce, but I wound up on that beach."

"I guess you couldn't make any money in another country, could you? I mean, they don't like foreigners taking the jobs, do they?"

"I wasn't worried about that. I thought I could always make a living."

"How? What would you do?"

"Well, there's this guy owes me a big tractor. A builder. I helped him out once when he was broke and he said, when he got back on his feet, he'd give me a tractor. And I know he got on his feet all right, but I never had any use for a tractor. He offered me cash, but I told him to hold it; someday I might really need it. So, I think if I owned a tractor, I could make a living almost anywhere."

"Why didn't you do it then—at that time?"

"I don't know. I didn't have anything against my own country. I liked the beach. I guess it was mainly laziness."

"Hey," she said quietly, "I think you've got a bite."

One of the lines was taut and the pole quivered sharply. He pulled it out of the sand, raised it experimentally, then began to reel in the line, moving toward the water as it shortened. Carol followed by fits and starts, keeping her distance. She could see a small fish flopping in the surf. Dan dropped the pole, waded into the water and lifted the catch.

"Yellowtail," he said. "Enough for dinner. Or do you want me to try for more?"

"No," she said. "I don't like the look on his face."

"He's to eat," Dan said, "not to make friends with." She shook her head sadly as she picked up their towels and started toward the house.

"Oh boy!" she said. "My big, strong, realistic hero!"

\* \* \* \*

In the night, he woke and she was not in the bed. He waited a short time, then got up and found her in the kitchen, in the dark, standing at the back window, sipping from a long drink. The whisky bottle stood open on the shelf.

"I couldn't sleep," she said.

She looked at him with defiance, then turned away. There was nothing to be seen through the window but the grotesque shapes of the seaside growth and, distantly, a glow of pink light over the town. He put his hand on her and she drew away, then returned.

"What you need," he said, "is a wardrobe. Look at you, not a stitch to your name."

She turned against his hand, then, with a sudden fury, set her glass down hard on the tile shelf. The glass shattered and the spilled liquid spread over the shelf and dripped down the cupboard doors below.

"Goddam it, I hate whisky!" she said.

He drew her away from the shelf and turned on a light.

"We'll switch to tequila," he said. "Better for you anyway."

"Oh God," she said.

He found a rag and began to clean up the shelf. She watched for a while, then pushed him away.

"I made it," she said. "I'll eat it."

"You'd better go back to bed."

"Please?" she said.

He looked at her with some concentration, then relinquished the rag and left her. When she returned to the bed, there was blood on her fingers.

"I cut myself on the glass," she said.

In the morning, he woke before her and there was dried blood on him. He stood by the bed for a long time, looking at her asleep, then he put on trunks and walked down on the beach and went for a swim. The sun was bright and the sky clear. He swam so far out, he could see into the harbor, and he rested there for some time, watching the harbor and the wheeling gulls and the bright sunlight on the sea around him.

# CHAPTER 10

In the town, they walked the dusty streets. There were stores displaying imported merchandise of quality, as well as curio shops crammed with a mixture of cheap souvenirs and original examples of Mexican handicraft; tin, silver, glass and pottery; and many dress shops, catering to both local and tourist customers.

"About that wardrobe," he said.

"You've spent enough money on me," she said.

She lingered over a display of casual and sportswear. "How would I look in one of those Mexican outfits?" she said.

"Fine," he said.

"They don't seem so expensive."

He took money from his wallet and gave it to her. "Why don't you look around," he said. "Get whatever you want and I'll meet you for lunch."

"All right. Where?"

"That hotel? It's only three or four blocks down. On the waterfront, remember?"

"Yes."

She hesitated, searching his face, started into the store, then turned back. He drew her aside, against the wall of the building, put his arms around her and kissed her.

"Ooh," she said, "it started bleeding. I could feel it."

"Want first aid?"

"No. It's only a little." She kissed his chin, stretching up to reach him. "When we separate," she said, "it's like I'll never see you again."

"I won't run out on you," he said.

"What if something should happen? Like an accident or something, and I couldn't make it to the hotel? Would you find me?"

"Yes," he said.

"Promise?"

"Yes."

She drew a long breath. "All right! Here I go."

She turned quickly and went into the store.

Outside the hotel, he was pacing back and forth. She had only one small package. "I'm sorry it took so long," she said. "I couldn't make up my mind. It was awful."

"What did you find?"

She looked guilty. "A couple of bikinis."

"That's all?"

"I couldn't make up my mind. Anyway, we're on the beach most of the time. Were you worried about me?"

"Yes and no."

"I'm sorry. Were you about to start looking for me?"

"In about three minutes."

She slipped her hand under his arm. "Look, let's not go to the hotel," she said. "Let's go home. I'll fix you a good lunch. Come on. I'll show you the bikinis, too."

"Stuffed?"

"Yes."

"All right."

Driving home in the truck, they had to wait at an intersection while a troop of thirty or forty men in uniform crossed at double time.

"What's that?" she said. "The army?"

"Police. I guess they're changing the shift."

"All those cops for one little town?"

"Well, this is a rough little town."

The officers cleared the intersection and they went on. She said nothing more till they reached the house. As he brought the truck to a stop, she began to unbutton her blouse.

"Come on!" she said.

Before he could get down to help her, she had seized her small package and left the truck and was running into the house. But when he got there, she was only sitting on the edge of the sofa, her blouse half open, holding the package with both hands on her knees and gazing into space.

"What is it?" he asked.

"I don't know," she said, looking around the room as if seeing it for the first time. "It just suddenly hit me—you know something? This is the first time in my life I ever had anything like a real home."

"With your sister?"

She blinked at him, then shook her head.

"No, and not anywhere else. There was always something wrong—sick. Now all of a sudden there's nothing wrong and I can't get used to it."

"You haven't had much time."

"A man isn't like that, is he? Wherever he is, that's home."

"I wouldn't say that. Some places are more like home than others."

"Is this like home for you?"

"Yes, it is."

"Because of me? Or because of the ocean, the beach?"

"All those things, I guess."

"But you could feel like home without me, couldn't you? If you were on the beach."

"It wouldn't be the same."

"How do you know? You didn't have much time to get used to me. Aside from the lovemaking—I mean, you don't have to get used to that, do you? A man, I mean?"

He cupped her chin in his hand and looked at her with tolerance. "You're getting to be quite a talker. Mucho conversation on an empty stomach."

"Yeah," she said. "Just let me slip into something comfortable."

She took her package into the bedroom and closed the door.

* * * *

In the kitchen, she was cleaning up after the lunch, when he excused himself to get into his trunks. Before leaving the room, he opened a small metal canister on the shelf under the cupboards and emptied into it some bills and change from his pockets. When he had gone, she dried her hands, opened the canister and looked into it. After a moment, she put her hand inside and fingered the contents, her lips moving. Then, without removing anything, she replaced the cover and went on with her work.

* * * *

He set up his fish poles on the beach, the baited hooks as far out as he could fling them, and they stood knee-deep in the cold surf. She looked down at herself, where a strip of adhesive tape showed between the top of the new bikini and her navel.

"Kind of spoils the effect, doesn't it?" she said.

He touched it gently. "What made you do that?"

"I don't know. Something came over me."

"Does it come over you often?"

"No. Take it off, huh?"

"We ought to make sure it's clean."

"Go ahead. Take it off."

He gripped a corner of the tape and peeled it off quickly. Her flesh winced, but her face was stoical, watching. A little blood welled from the small wound on her belly.

"I didn't do much, did I?" she said. "No guts."

He went down on his knees to examine the cut. She put her hands on his face and thrust herself at him suddenly. He lost his balance and fell backward and she tumbled over him into the water. She screamed at the cold shock and thrashed about, gasping. When he caught and lifted her, she was choking. He brushed her wet hair out of her face and carried her up on the dry sand, where she sprawled in the sun while he tended his lines. When he returned, she held out her arms and he embraced her, but he was frowning.

"What's the matter, my hero?" she said. "I'm a regular nuisance, huh?"

"You're—impulsive," he said. "I have to watch you every minute, just to keep you alive."

"It's not me," she said. "It's because the glass was so sharp and the water was so cold."

"I understand," he said.

"I don't want to die."

"All right."

"Promise?"

"Sure. Just stick with me."

She raised herself on her hands. "There goes another one."

A freighter was moving out of the harbor, bearing southwest. They could see movements on her decks and her flag in the breeze.

"Where's it going?" she said.

"Who knows? Honolulu, Guam, Tahiti—"

"Stop! I can't stand it."

"You'd like to go to those far-off places?"

"Wouldn't everybody?"

"Everybody's a lot of people."

She moved suddenly, butting him with her shoulder and one hip so that he fell away from her.

"Hey!" she said.

He looked where she was pointing and one of the fish poles had been torn from its shallow socket in the sand and was being dragged toward the surf. The long, silver line stretched far out and was quivering violently. By the time he reached the pole, the line had gone slack. It had run out to the limit of the reel and as he began to wind it in, the line snaking limply out of the surf, she came to join him.

"What happened?" she said.

He shrugged. "Little fish on hook. Big fish grab little fish—kaput."

"A shark?"

"Don't know. Could be."

"You're not going swimming off this beach again."

"Well, not this afternoon."

"Not tomorrow, either, or the day after that."

"It didn't have to be a shark," he said. "There are all kinds of fish."

"I don't care," she said.

He was examining the cut end of the line.

"Not too far out," he said. "I wonder what I had on there?"

He put the pole down and went to the other, upright in the sand. He reeled the line in and it was intact, though the bait was gone.

"I never really cared a lot for fishing anyway," he said. "Maybe we could go out to dinner."

She put her arms around him.

"We don't have to," she said. "Got muchas canned goods. Let's just be alone, private, please? *Por favor.*"

"You're getting very linguistic," he said.

"I don't want to be just another tourista."

"All right, señorita," he said, "let's see a little action."

He loosened the tie on her hip that held the bikini in place, and it fell away. She stepped out of it, snatched it up and ran toward the house, her buttocks churning in the labored stride. He picked up the fishing tackle and bait can and followed, not hurrying.

When he came out of the shower, she was on the bed, naked, waiting. He leaned over her, kissing her erect nipples and her hands moved over him.

"Listen," she said, "I take it all back about wanting to be a mermaid. When you stop and think about it, that's really nothing, that no-crotch business."

She squirmed under him. "You want to watch that—eating between meals," she said. "You'll spoil your appetite!"

"I don't think so," he said. "I'm a good feeder."

"Yes—oh yes!"

\* \* \* \*

In the bedroom, there was a corner window that gave on the beach. She was sitting up in the bed, looking out the window, and she began to shiver, though the room was still warm. The sun had set, but there was a lingering twilight. She folded her arms tightly over her breasts, but the shivering continued. She looked down at him asleep beside her. He smiled in his sleep and reached out. She sat still, watching his hand grope over her knee, hip, flank. He woke, as if in search of response, and raised himself on his elbow.

"Carol—"

"Listen," she said, "if all of a sudden I had to go away—if I wasn't around anymore—would you miss me?"

"You talk like you lost your mind."

"I mean it. There are girls everywhere, a dime a dozen."

"Sure."

"All the same basic construction."

"I guess so. How would I know?"

"You know what I mean. So why would you miss me?"

He scratched his head, then his chest.

"I'm used to you," he said.

She ground her knee against his hip.

"Ouch," he said. "What do you want me to say? I love you?"

"Oh God," she said.

"Anybody can say 'I love you.' A guy gets too excited and nothing else works, he can say 'I love you.'"

"I know, I know."

"Why do you want me to say a thing whether you can believe it or not?"

"If you said it, I'd believe it. But I don't want you to say it."

"You want me not to say it?"

"You son of a bitch—I didn't bring it up about 'I love you.' That was you."

"A figure of speech," he said.

"Listen," she said, "were you ever in the guardhouse or the stockade, or whatever it is, when you were in the service?"

"What kind of a question is that? No, I never was."

"I just wondered what it was like."

"It wouldn't be fun."

"I couldn't stand it, to be shut up somewhere, locked up."

"Yes, you could. You can stand anything."

"No, I couldn't. If I thought I was going to be locked up, I'd kill myself."

He held her as if to smother her. "Come on, between us, we'll talk ourselves to death."

Her fists ground at his chest, but then she quieted and stretched out along him, her hands clinging to his ribs, her mouth at his throat.

"Dan, listen," she said. "We could take that trip."

"Uh-huh."

She lay still with him, saying nothing while the twilight faded. Then she stirred restlessly. "It's so dark."

"Do you want me to turn on a light? Would you rather get up?"

"No. Listen—there's a boat we can take, a freighter from Panama. The captain's name is Lorca."

He said nothing.

"The reason I was so long meeting you today was," she said, "this Captain Lorca tried to pick me up. Right on the street. I was looking in a window and he came along and started talking. He speaks good English. So I didn't want to make a big scene on the street, so I kept him talking—about himself, which was easy. When he said he had this boat, it hit me. I asked him if he ever took any passengers and he gave me some more of his pitch, and I asked where he was going from here, and he said south, Mexico, Costa Rica, Peru. So I said that my—uh—husband and I were thinking about a trip, just to see what he would say. Well, the husband thing kind of cooled him off, but he said he had accommodations on the boat, if we were interested. So that's how I found out about him."

"How long will he be in port?"

"I don't know. A few days."

After a while he ran his hand slowly over her hip and thigh to her knee and back again.

"Let's go find something to eat," he said.

He was dressed before her, waiting in the kitchen. She wore the dark skirt he had given her and a blouse and sweater. She had left her hair down and applied makeup sparingly and she had the little girl look, as during the first days on the beach. She watched him take money from the canister and said nothing and they left the house and drove to the hotel where they had met for lunch. After they were seated, he excused himself.

At the hotel desk, he asked for a telegraph form and he was there for some time, composing a message and waiting patiently as it was read back to him in slow, conscientious English by a smartly dressed clerk.

"'If I find suitable, medium heavy cat reasonable—' That is, 'cat,' señor?"

"Si. Tractor. Bulldozer."

"*Si*, okay. '…reasonable, can you purchase for delivery in Ensenada?'"

"That is correct."

"And the signature, señor is, 'Dan Low—"

"Dan Lowry. Yes. A night letter, please."

"Night letter. You are registered at the hotel, señor?"

"No. I'll stop in tomorrow some time, if I may use the hotel address?"

"Certainly, señor. *Gracias.*"

*"Muchas gracias."*

When he went back to the dining room, there were two long-stemmed glasses on the table.

"I ordered Margaritas. Is that all right?" she said.

"That's fine," he said.

A small combination of guitars and violins began to play. They raised their glasses to each other, but their eyes failed to meet squarely—though he smiled and after a moment, tentatively, she smiled too—as if the movements of their eyes were restricted by some secret hinge.

# CHAPTER 11

They sat with Captain Lorca in a booth in a quiet, air-conditioned bar. It was three o'clock in the afternoon and there were no other customers. The bartender was half asleep on a stool at the end of the bar.

Lorca was massive for a Latin, with thick, black hair, white teeth, and a hooked nose that had been broken at some time and had knit badly. He wore blue dungarees and a blue yachting cap and his arms swelled from the short sleeves of a striped T-shirt. He and Carol were drinking whisky and Dan was drinking coffee.

"I can give you passage to Guayaquil," Lorca was saying, "for one thousand dollars, señor. For the two of you. You would have a clean room, with bath. The food on my ship is very good. I see to it myself."

"When do you expect to put in at Guayaquil?" Dan asked.

Lorca shrugged. "In about one week, señor, from the time we depart from Ensenada. I don't know exactly—there is some delay here with the cargo."

"A matter of days?"

"*Si, tres*—three, four days."

"Will you be fully loaded here in Ensenada?"

"Who knows?" Lorca smiled. "I can't stay in port forever. There is the expense of the crew—"

"Will you have room to transport a tractor—bulldozer?"

"Yes, I am sure." He smiled with the white teeth. "You own a tractor, señor?"

"I'm buying one here, in Ensenada."

Lorca nodded. "You have nothing to worry about," he said. "You can make a good profit on a tractor anywhere in South America."

"You will be able to deliver it in Guayquill—?"

"*Si.* No trouble. Very small duty. I can arrange it."

"How much for the freight, roughly?"

"Two, three hundred dollars, depending on the weight."

Dan looked at the girl, who sat with her glass between her hands, not looking at either of them. He looked at Lorca again.

"Do you want a deposit?"

Lorca showed his teeth. "No hurry, señor. You and the señora will want to see the accommodations. Any time after four o'clock. You can reach the ship by the harbor service, or I can send a boat for you."

"We won't impose on your time, Captain. *Muchas gracias*."

"Nothing." He slid out of the booth and stood, a huge man, with his teeth very white in his brown face. "If you will tell me about the tractor, when you have the necessary papers, I will make the arrangements."

"Thank you."

"Nothing, señor." He turned to Carol, bowed and smiled. "Señora, good afternoon. *Hasta la vista*."

Her lips moved, murmuring, *"Hasta la vista*, Captain Lorca."

Lorca strode away. In passing, he tossed a large silver coin on the bar. The dozing bartender jumped to his feet, startled. Lorca looked back at the booth, laughing, waved and went out.

Dan drank some of his coffee.

"He looks like he's made up for a pirate," Carol said.

"He's a pirate all right, but not as bad as he might be."

She looked at him, sipping her drink.

"The difference between a reasonable fare to Guayaquil and the amount Lorca is asking will make a nice wad in his pocket."

"Maybe you could have haggled with him," she said.

He looked at her and she looked away.

"Would you like to go shopping?" he asked.

"Not if everything is going to cost so much," she said.

"I didn't mean that."

"All right," she said, "but I don't feel like shopping."

"Would you mind staying here for an hour or so, while I see about the tractor?"

"No, I wouldn't mind. It's nice here."

"I'll come back for you and we'll go see the ship."

"All right."

"Do you have enough money?"

She looked into her purse. "Yes," she said. "Plenty. I won't do anything extravagant."

His mouth tightened as he got out of the booth and turned away. She reached and caught his sleeve and he turned back and leaned over her. Her eyes slid to glance at the now quiescent bartender, then returned. She lifted her face and he kissed her. She put her hand on him.

"I'm sorry about being a bitch," she said.

He kissed her cheek and would have left her, but she clung to him. "Forgive me?"

"What else?"

"Dan, I love you."

"Watch it. You'll start something we can't finish in a public place, even in Ensenada."

"Just to make you hurry back," she said.

He kissed her on the mouth and walked away.

She gazed after him through the open door to the sunlit street, then shifted her eyes to the bartender, who had gotten up and was polishing glasses.

"*Si, señora,*" he said. "Whisky?"

She held her hand flat above the glass.

"*Dos,*" she said. "Double."

"*Si, señora.*"

Captain Lorca came in, bowed with excessive courtesy and asked permission to join her.

"Yes, Captain," she said. "My husband will be back soon. He went to see about the tractor."

"Very good," he said. "Have you been married a long time, señora? No, you're too young for a long time. This is a honeymoon trip?"

"In a way," she said.

Lorca ordered a drink and inspected her at leisure, till she turned her face to avoid his eyes.

"You forgot your rings, señora."

She looked at her left hand.

"I take them off when I do the dishes," she said. "I forgot to put them on again."

He took her hand in his and his thumb stroked the back of it lightly.

"Lovely hand," he said. "You are a lovely blonde woman. Señor— your husband is a lucky man."

"You like blondes, Captain?"

"Who does not?"

She withdrew her hand.

"Excuse me," Lorca said, settling back. "I forget myself. When I approached you on the street yesterday, I did not know you were married."

"I understand," she said.

"You were not wearing the rings yesterday either," he said.

"Well, I do a lot of dishes, Captain."

"*Si, señora.*"

When Dan came in, Lorca rose to greet him.

"I had business in the town and I thought I could escort you to the boat personally."

"All right," Dan said. He handed Lorca some documents. "I own the tractor," he said. "For shipping, there are papers the dealer has to prepare. He'll have them tomorrow some time."

"Very good," Lorca said. "The dealer is—?"

Dan told him the name.

"I will see to it," Lorca said. "Would you like to visit the ship now?"

"Thank you," Dan said.

He helped Carol out of the booth and the three of them left the bar.

They were undressing for bed at three o'clock in the morning.

"How did you like the boat?" she asked.

"It appears to be seaworthy."

"Are you angry about something?"

"No."

"You don't have to go if you don't want to. I'm sure Captain Lorca will give your thousand dollars back."

"I only gave him five hundred, by way of good faith."

"Well, if you're not sore about anything, what's the matter?"

"Nothing. I guess it's only that most of the afternoon and evening is a long time to spend with Captain Lorca."

"We'll be spending more time than that with him if we go on the boat."

"I know."

"Didn't you enjoy the dinner, and the show?"

"I guess I did."

"I thought it was very generous of Captain Lorca."

"Yes," he said.

She was sitting on the edge of the bed, watching him. "Maybe you disapprove of that kind of a show—striptease and all that."

"No."

"I didn't think it was so great. I heard they ran wide open down here."

"There were several women in the place, touristas, and it was still early when we left."

"Have you ever seen one in Mexico that was wide open?"

"Yes."

"What was it like?"

"Well, it was more or less like tonight, only more so."

"Does that do anything for you? I mean, that kind of a show—erotic?"

"What do you mean?"

He started past her to leave the room and she caught at him. He stopped and stood, facing her.

"You know what I mean. Does it *do* anything for you?"

"I suppose so, in a way."

"But not much, huh?"

"Not a hell of a lot, no."

"Do I do anything for you?"

"Always."

"Like—this? Wait a minute, stand still…)

"Ouch."

"Excuse me. I'm sorry."

He went out and when he returned, she was in bed. He got in beside her and lay on his back, blinking in the dark.

"Did Lorca annoy you?" he asked, "in that bar, before I came?"

"No," she said. "He was very nice and a perfect gentleman. He explained that when he tried to pick me up the day before, he didn't know I was married. Is that what was bothering you? Me being there with Captain Lorca when you got back?"

"Only if he gave you trouble."

"No, he didn't give me any trouble."

She turned in the bed and he reached for her.

"Come on," he said. "I'll give you some trouble."

"Yes," she said.

* * * *

In the morning, a thick fog lay over the beach and they could hear muffled whistles and bells distantly. From the window, they could see only as far as the surf and nothing of the town. By the time they finished breakfast, the fog had begun to lift, but the sky remained overcast until afternoon.

"I want to see about selling the truck," he said, "and you ought to do that shopping."

"Well, I—what should I—?"

"You should have a raincoat, walking shoes, a heavy sweater, some wool dresses."

"All right," she said. "You sound like we're going to Alaska—or San Francisco."

"Wherever you go, the main thing to prepare for is to keep warm."

"All right. You keep me warm, lover."

In town, it was hot and the dust was cloying. He stopped to let her out in the shopping section. She left the truck reluctantly and held him with her eyes.

"If you sell the truck," she said, "how will we get home?"

"I won't turn it over till we're ready to go," he said. "I want to get an idea what they'll pay. I may want to take it back to San Diego and sell it there."

"Well—good luck," she said. "Where will you meet me?"

"The hotel," he said. "I don't know how long I'll be."

"Tell me again what I should buy."

"Raincoat, shoes, sweater, wool dresses."

She repeated it after him, checking them off on her fingers.

"See how helpless I am?" she said.

"You'll be all right," he said.

"Yes, but hurry back anyway."

She waited on the curb as he got into the truck and pulled away. Not till he was out of sight did she turn and walk slowly down the street.

\* \* \* \*

He found her in the cocktail lounge at the hotel. She had several packages and offered to open them on the spot, to prove she had been a good girl, but he said he could wait till they got home.

The weather had changed with the fog and it was steaming hot on the beach, but the house was cool. She showed him what she had bought and he approved it.

"Did you make a deal for the truck?" she asked.

"I found a dealer who'll give me four hundred dollars for it—in pesos. I could beat that a little in San Diego, but not enough to pay for the trip."

"Then I guess we're all set."

"I guess so."

"Except for one thing," she said.

"What?"

"You don't really want to go."

"What makes you say that?"

"Because it's true."

"I want to go wherever you go."

"We don't have to look at it like the end of the world. Captain Lorca said you could make a good deal on the tractor anywhere. We can take a cruise and sell the tractor any time you want to come home, okay?"

"Sure," he said.

"But if you don't want to go…"

"Isn't that about where we started?" he said.

She stared at him for a few seconds, then turned away.

"Yes, I guess it is," she said.

He undressed, put on his trunks, and took the fishing tackle down on the beach. After he had the lines out, he went for a swim and returned to sit on the sand. The fog came in before the sun went down and the girl, waiting in the house, watched from the bedroom window. He was there until nearly dark, until she could barely see him in the fog, but when he came up, she saw he had not caught any fish.

"Sorry, no luck," he said, when he came in, and went on into the bedroom.

He was dressing after a shower when she came to the bedroom door. The overhead light was on and it illuminated her harshly, accentuating the spareness of her bone structure, as if she were a doll made of wire with bits of apparent flesh attached here and there.

"Do you want something from a can?" she asked. "Or would you rather eat out?"

"Which would you rather?"

"I don't care."

He finished dressing before he spoke again. She waited in the doorway. When he reached for a necktie, she went into the room, opened the closet and selected a dress.

"Let's go somewhere," he said.

"All right," she said.

\* \* \* \*

In the morning, the fog lifted early. He was down on the beach with his fishing gear before she woke. When she came out, he was sitting near the upright poles, his arms on his knees, looking out to sea.

"Any luck yet?" she said.

"Not yet."

She spread a towel and sat down a little way off and rubbed suntan lotion on her arms and face.

"What are you thinking about?" she said.

He shrugged and ran his hands through his hair.

"Are you thinking about the Old Man?"

"I wasn't," he said.

She was somewhat behind him on the towel, watching him now with an intent curiosity. "The Old Man is here," she said. "In town."

He turned his head slowly and looked at her.

"I saw him yesterday," she said. "When I was shopping."

"Did he see you?"

"No, I don't think so."

"Didn't you speak to him?"

"He was on the other side of the street. He was just going into some store when I saw him."

He looked away toward the water. After a minute, he got up, pulled one of the poles from the sand and began methodically to reel in the line.

* * * *

In the bedroom, he was dressing and she hovered, watching him in a secret way, avoiding his eyes. As if he became aware of her only gradually, his movements slowed, finally stopped and he sat on the bed with a shoe dangling from one hand.

"What happened to Freddie Benedict?" he said.

She looked at him for a long time, then turned away to the window.

"I killed him," she said. "I guess I killed him."

"How? How did you kill him?"

"I shot him."

"Where did you get the gun?"

"It was his, I guess. It was right there."

"Ever shoot a gun before?"

"No."

"What kind of a gun was it?"

"I don't know. Just a gun."

"Was it a big gun, with a long barrel?"

"No, a small one. A pistol, I think."

"How did you do it? Exactly how with the pistol?"

"I—he was sitting in a chair—the gun was on a table—"

"Wait. I mean, how did you hold the gun? With one hand?"

"No, both hands."

"He came after you and you grabbed the gun and shot him?"

"No! No, no, no, you can't make it out like, that."

He turned his face slightly, looking toward the window. She came to him and put her hands on his shoulders and after a minute, he put one hand on her hip lightly and looked up at her. "All right," he said, "why? Why did you shoot him?"

"Because—he killed my sister."

"With his own hands?"

"No."

"Tell me why."

She was a long time starting and he waited in silence.

"It starts with the accident, in San Francisco. I was sixteen then and it was so horrible. It was a stupid accident, with a car; it was my father's fault. When I went to see her in the hospital, she was all wrapped up in bandages. I couldn't see any of her face. She couldn't talk. I would talk and she would write on a slate. 'Don't cry,' she wrote, 'I'll be all right.' And she wrote, 'As soon as I'm all right, I'll take you back to LA with me.' But when she was all right, my mother got sick and I didn't get to LA till after high school.

"I hadn't seen her for almost two years and it was a shock. She wore a veil at first, when she went back to work, but she stopped that. The people she worked for were wonderful—she was an accountant; she was so good, they paid her full salary all the time she was in the hospital, and she got me a job at the same place, a clerical job. I didn't know much. She made me go to night school so I could learn how to do something. She tried to get me to go out, too, lead a normal life. I liked having dates all right, but as soon as the guy would start anything, I'd panic. I never told her about that. She had enough."

She moved away from him and returned to the window.

"She had these oddball friends—quirky, you know? They would be hipped on something and they'd sit around and talk about it all the whole goddam night long. I resented them because they came between us. I was so dependent on her. I was jealous of them."

"I understand," he said.

"Anyway—some of them were nudists, so that's how we got started on that. It was at the nudist camp we first heard about Freddie Benedict."

"Benedict was a nudist?"

"No, but some of these people knew him. They introduced him to my sister. By the time I met him, they were pretty far along. It was too late."

She fell silent and he prompted her.

"Too late?" he said.

"You see—I didn't know how lonely she was. I didn't know what it would mean to her, to be in love."

She turned to look at him. In the bright sunlight, her hair had a cottony texture.

"What?" he said.

"She let herself fall in love with him—Freddie Benedict."

She came back and knelt on the floor and crossed her arms on his knees.

"Fantastic, huh?" she said. "Talk about quirky—he was the champ. But you get where my sister was, you can't tell the difference anymore."

He could feel the bed shaking and he ran his hands down over her back, stroking her.

"I could tell something had happened," she said. "She was different, but she didn't tell me about it until one day, she said, 'Let's go down to the beach over the weekend.' So I thought we'd stay in some motel, you know, but we went to his house and that's where we stayed.

"There were other girls there—more or less misfits, like my sister. One was very fat, like a fat girl in the circus. Another poor kid was ordinary size, but very homely, with warts on her face. One of the others had a spinal thing that had crippled her. It looked kind of funny at first, but I could see they were having a good time and when I met him—Benedict—he was friendly and nice and real sweet to my sister. He was just a rich, middle-aged guy giving a party. That's what it was like, a house party, without glamour girls. But not as bad as it sounds—it wasn't an orgy exactly. It was a nice, fun weekend and I enjoyed it." She put her head down on her arms. "I didn't know what was going on—that Freddie Benedict was making love to my sister—for kicks. Just for kicks."

She looked up.

"That son of a bitch let her believe it. She was going to be Missus Freddie Benedict, for real. For one short, passionate year, he let her believe it. He bought her books, clothes, a new car. They were even going round looking at houses."

She moved on her knees, as if to go away, then returned.

Well," she said, "he could do it to most girls and it would be tough, but they asked for it and it happens all the time. But my sister was different and he knew it. He knew!

"Listen, the night he dropped the sky on her, he called another girl, a long-time friend, and told her he was going to do it. He asked her to come and stay with my sister as long as necessary because he was afraid she would take it pretty hard. But it didn't work out—I mean, she took it hard all right, but the rest of it—the cooling off period—went all to hell. She gave the goodwill kid the slip and she drove her car, south, a hundred miles an hour. She drove in a straight line and she didn't make the first curve. She didn't even try."

After a while, he said, "That was over a year ago."

"Yes. So why did it take me so long? Is that what you mean?"

"That's not what I said."

"All right—the next thing, I lost my job. They only kept me on there because of my sister. Also, I was drinking a lot. If I could have stopped drinking and learned how to handle the ass-pinchers, I think I could have held some kind of a job. But without my sister, I was nothing. But nothing!"

She was silent, and he said, "Did you always feel like nothing?"

"Without my sister, yes. Anyway, things went from bad to worse. I couldn't pay the rent and had to move in with another girl, a real oddball. She didn't drink or smoke and she didn't approve of anybody else doing it and she lived on grapes and raisins. I tried to get work as a model, but I was too small for fashion—or almost anything respectable, so somebody tipped me to a couple of photographers and I started—whatever I could get. Whether you know it or not, the pay isn't much, but at least I could get away from that grape-eater. And I kept on drinking and hanging around with characters and then one day I ran into him—Benedict. Well, not exactly; he looked me up to see if he could help me.

"I was pretty desperate. The day before, I'd had a big fight with one of the photographers, and I knew I wouldn't get any work for a while. I was down to about twenty dollars and the whisky was about gone and I was sick to my stomach and the rent was due on this lousy cheap room in Hollywood, and that's the time he picked to look me up.

"He was his usual charming self, of course. He said he wanted me to come down to the beach and rest and think things over and get back on my feet and that jazz. And I asked him what it would cost, this little rest cure, and he said nothing. And I didn't have anywhere else to go. So I went with him, just as I was. I didn't have any clothes worth keeping anyway. I left a note for the landlady and told her to do whatever she wanted with the stuff. I said I was moving in with a friend in another town.

"And we went down there, to his place, just the two of us. He had a colored maid that worked for his sister, too, but his sister was sick—she's a lush—so even the maid wasn't there. All the time I was there, nobody but the two of us. He was very nice to me at first, and there was no problem with him, no physical problem, I mean. It was part of his quirk. He took me over to Fashion Square and gave me five hundred dollars and told me to get whatever I wanted and if it came to more than five hundred, to charge it to him. But I couldn't make up my mind about anything and the only thing I saw that I wanted was that evening dress—the one you saw me in—and the pumps and lingerie and the little bag. When I gave him the change, he laughed about it, but it didn't matter to him. We weren't going out anywhere.

"On top of the house, he had this solarium—all glass, but frosted; plenty of sunlight, but nobody could look in. There were big pads on the floor and cushions and a magazine rack and a wet bar. We spent most of our time there during the day 'wrestling with the demon rum,' he said. I put on a show for him, whining and begging and panting, but it wasn't really so rugged. I wasn't a real lush—what the AA would call a lush.

"So—the good food and sunshine and I guess not having anything to worry about began to make me feel better. All this time, of course, neither of us mentioned my sister, or any of those other poor kids, and he kept building me up, telling me how 'lovely' I was. 'You're too lovely to destroy yourself,' he kept saying.

"He was really land of fun to be with. He was an artist, more or less; he was a good cartoonist anyway. He had a parlor game that most people got a bang out of. He had these two dummies—mannequins—life-size, one male and female and he would make them into people, with makeup and wigs and clothing—he could make the dummy look like anybody in the world—Marilyn Monroe, Joan Crawford, Marlon Brando, Winston Churchill. He was very quick at it; one minute it was a dummy and the next minute—somebody!

"So this night we were sitting around after dinner, drinking champagne—because he had dried me out and he would let me drink wine—and he started the business with the dummies. I had been there five days and I was relaxed and not worried about anything, except that I was hitting the champagne pretty hard. I would give him a request and he would see how fast he could make the dummy into that person. And finally, I was feeling kind of silly. 'Make the dummy like me,' I said. And he thought it over for a couple of minutes and said, 'All right, give me your dress. I don't know if I have any hair like yours.' So I took off my dress and he put it on the dummy and went to work. It took him a lot longer than usual and when he finished, it didn't really look much like me and he wasn't happy about it.

"Then, to cheer him up, I picked out somebody—Elizabeth Taylor, I think—I knew he wouldn't have any trouble with and he came up with an idea of his own. 'The hell with the dummy,' he said, 'let me make *you* into Liz Taylor.' So by then I was ready to go for most anything and he found a slinky kind of dress for me and sat me down by the makeup table and went to work. He wouldn't let me watch him in the mirror while he did it. 'You have to wait till it's done,' he said, 'or it spoils the effect for you.' So he made me into Liz Taylor and it was pretty good. Then we did some others, one after the other and he got warmed up to it and was doing great and finally I couldn't think of any more people."

She wiped her nose with the palm of her hand and swallowed, long and painfully. When she spoke again, her voice was low and flat, as if she were reciting a lesson prepared under duress.

"So he said he had an idea, and I said what was it and he said to be patient and he would surprise me. He gave it the big build-up, walking back and peering at me from all sides and squinting and fussing around with his makeup, and then he got started. I tried to sneak a look in the mirror, but he wouldn't let me. So I sat there and let him go ahead and he worked quite a while. When he finished, he stood back to inspect his work, but he still wouldn't let me look. He gave it a few finishing touches. He did something with my hair and he had already put me back in my own dress. And then finally he said, 'All right, it's the best I can do, honey.' And I looked in the mirror, and what he had done to me—he had made me into my sister. A monster. I couldn't believe it. I stared at this awful-looking thing and I couldn't believe it was me. I won't try to describe it, because you wouldn't believe it anyway. It was horrible—so horrible.

"When I looked around at him, he was standing there kind of chuckling and nodding his head. I yelled something at him and he looked surprised. I threw the makeup box at him and he backed away. 'Listen, it was a joke.' he said. And I kept on yelling at him and throwing things and he ducked out of the room.

"So there was a small bathroom off this—studio he had—and I went in there and stripped and cleaned myself up; it took a long, long time and I couldn't believe I really had gotten it all off, even when I looked in the mirror. I must have washed my face fifty times. Then I got very sick and I didn't bother to clean that up. I went in the living room and he was sitting there in his favorite chair, just sitting, and he started to say how sorry he was and I said I was leaving. He got kind of sore about it then and made some nasty remarks and I made some back at him. And he took my purse out of my hand and opened it and put a thousand dollar bill in it and gave it back to me. 'I'm sorry,' he said, 'but one thing you have to have around Freddie Benedict is a sense of humor.' And I told him what he could do and started out.

"Well, I had to walk around the chair he was sitting in to get to the door and behind the chair was this table and the gun was lying there on the table. And just about the time I got behind him—he didn't even look around to say goodnight—my mouth tasted terrible from the champagne and being sick and my stomach was going crazy and I couldn't get that goddam horrible face out of my mind and I picked up the gun and pointed it at the back of his head and shot him. I didn't mean to shoot him more than once—I mean I didn't really mean to shoot him at all—but it was one of those guns that had a—when I pulled the trigger, it just kept shooting, and it had a—what—a kick? It almost flew out of my hand, so I dropped it and went out. And I started walking. I walked down to the highway and just kept walking and I got to there—that beach and couldn't walk anymore and I sat down on the rock and then you were coming up the beach and—that's the way it was."

She was kneeling, with her face on her arms on his knees and she pushed herself away and got to her feet and started away. Then she turned and found her way back to him and stood in front of him. He looked at her for a long time and then he put his shoe on the floor and his foot in the shoe and tied it. She went down on her knees again and he put his hands on her arms. She crawled close to him and put her forehead against his chest.

"What are you going to do?" she asked.

"I don't know. What do you want me to do?"

"It's not up to me. You're the judge. That's what your name means, doesn't it? Dan the judge."

"That was my father's idea—it was probably a joke, a subtle joke."

"If your father was alive now, would you ask him what to do?"

"I might. I probably would."

"What would he say?"

"How do I know? He would probably tell me to bring you to see him. And he'd think of something."

"Something like what?"

"Well, he was a lawyer. If I asked him to take your case, he would probably take it. But he would have certain commitments to the courts, the system. You would give yourself up and he'd try to get bail set for you, but that might be denied. And he would start working up a defense—"

"And all this time—I'd be in jail?"

"It wouldn't be so long—I don't know, a few weeks."

"A few weeks. And then what?"

"You'd go on trial and he would defend you. He would do the best he could. He was a good lawyer, I think."

"What if I didn't have any defense? What could he do?"

"He would get you the best break he could. Maybe probation, then you wouldn't have to serve time."

"Do you think he could get me probation?"

"No. I think he would have to get you off altogether or settle for a minimum sentence, like five years to life, I think you would get out in maybe three years."

"Three years. But maybe more, a lot more."

"I wouldn't think so. Not for this—unpremediated, with provocation—no."

"Who's going to pay for all this? Even your father couldn't do it for nothing."

"We would work that out. I would arrange to pay him."

"But your father is dead."

He put his arms around her and kissed her. He opened his mouth as if to say something, then closed it silently. He picked her up and put her on the bed and paced the floor for about five minutes. She lay still looking up at him.

"I have to go into town for a while," he said. "Do you want to come with me?"

"No," she said. "Are you going to see the Old Man?"

"Yes, because we had a money transaction and if anything went wrong with it, I'll have to fix it up before we can go."

Her eyes closed and opened again.

"All right," she said. "I'll wait."

"I'll come back," he said.

"Yes," she said.

He went out. She lay on the bed till she heard the truck start, then got up and went to the window. She was at the window for a while and then she went back to the bed and lay down.

# CHAPTER 12

At the hotel, he called from the desk and waited for some time but got no answer. He looked around the hotel carefully, then left it and began to search the town, doggedly, door by door. It was four o'clock in the afternoon when he found the Old Man in the bar where he had met Captain Lorca and made the arrangements.

There were several customers in the room, but the Old Man sat apart, in a booth toward the rear. The level of the long drink in front of him was still high in the glass. He wore a sport shirt, open at the neck and a light-colored leisure jacket and his glasses. A folded newspaper lay on the table beside his glass.

"What is it, Jack?" Dan asked.

The Old Man took off his glasses and held them in both hands.

"Sit down," he said. "I'll buy you a drink."

After a moment, Dan sat down across from him. "Whisky and water," he said, "if you will have one on me."

The creases deepened around the old Man's eyes, then flattened. The bartender brought Dan's whisky and went away.

"What are you going to do?" the Old Man asked.

"Everybody asks me that," Dan said.

The Old Man sipped at his drink, put his glasses on and took them off.

"They're looking for her now, by name," he said. "They know who she is."

"Have they connected us?"

"I think not. But soon."

"Is that why you came?"

"Yes, I guess that's the biggest part of it."

They drank for a while, separately, as if each were alone in the booth. It was Dan who broke the silence.

"Did they give you the money all right, at the Federal Savings?"

"What's that?" the Old Man said. Then, "Oh, yes, that will be all right."

"How did you get down here?" Dan asked. "You don't drive."

"I took the bus."

Dan's face twisted, as if in pain.

"You took the bus? A Mexican bus?"

The Old Man shrugged. "It's not an unpleasant trip. Leisurely. Man has a chance to look around, think."

Dan picked up his glass, then set it aside and laid his hands flat on the table. "What do you want from me? What can I do?"

"I don't know. What do you want from yourself?"

"I want to be wherever this girl is."

The Old Man looked at him with a disbelief he tried to congeal. "How do you propose to manage it?"

"We have some plans."

"Where can you possibly go? Dan, there's no place in the world—"

"We'll try."

The lean, dry fingers fumbled at the folded newspaper. He pushed it across the table for Dan to read, pointing out the place. Dan read, looked up and shrugged.

"They don't know where she is now," he said. "Mexico's a big country. They have to depend on the Mexican police. I think we'll be gone before they make it." He tried to meet the Old Man's eyes, failed and looked into his glass. "Unless somebody turns us in," he said.

The Old Man winced. Dan's hand lifted, as if to touch the other, then dropped limply.

"I'm sorry," he said.

The Old Man folded his arms on the table.

"No time to indulge in sensitivity," he said. "Will you come to the hotel with me? We can talk more easily."

"I can't leave her alone so long," Dan said. "She breaks down quickly."

"All right. Listen, my friend, what is it with the girl? What is it for you?"

"I—have a responsibility for her. It was my own doing. She put herself in my hands. What should I do? I brought her this far—should I tell her 'All right, this is the end of the line; it's too hot for me'?"

The Old Man said nothing, but watched him steadily with a kind of inexorable expectation.

"And also," Dan said quietly, "I love her."

"You love her," the Old Man said. "How long do you think a life is? A few weeks? This—love—is in your hose! What will you do when it runs dry? Or looks around for another garden—or the garden this girl is leaves you?"

"I'm committed!"

"You're committed by a series of events! You're a victim!"

"No, I made my own choice."

The Old Man smiled suddenly, gently. "Out of your own mouth," he said. "You're a man of reason whether you like it or not. I think we're getting somewhere."

Dan moved brusquely, as if to go.

"Wait," the Old Man said. "You feel now you can live by your guts. For a while, all right; you're in good supply. But what are you going to do with your head? Cut it off? You have a memory longer than your life. I don't know how it works, call it 'racial.' You were born with a commitment already in operation, continuous. Quote, 'a responsibility to the human race,' unquote. Out of your own mouth."

Dan gestured impatiently.

"Listen," the Old Man said. "I'm not against this girl. God knows, I'm not against love. And you know, or ought to, that if I were choosing up sides, you would be on my team. But right now, I don't think you've altogether shaped up. I don't think you've asked the key question, of yourself or anybody else." He raised his hand as Dan opened his mouth. "Hang on, you can listen a few minutes to an old man.

"I don't claim any exclusive on this—you know it as well as I do, in your bones. Look, one characteristic of the human being is his ability to project an image, create a fiction by which he may appear to be something he maybe not quite is—or vice versa. Not a wholly bad thing—easier to deal with the image than the real thing. But what if it becomes necessary to get beyond the image, pierce the mask? Not over a long time, as an analyst or cross-examiner works, but right now, pronto? The best means I know of is the device of the key question."

He stopped as Dan's eyes shifted. Captain Lorca came into the tavern and stood at the bar. Dan looked at him for a moment, then returned to the Old Man.

"Maybe I'm repeating myself," the Old Man said. "We've discussed this before?"

"I don't think so," Dan said. "Go ahead."

"Well—the key question doesn't always occur to you at once, but it comes along. May not seem to make sense—totally unrelated to the context—startling revelation, especially in one's self—everybody his own con man. But to get back to it—something is usually missing from every story. I once dealt with a man who was trying to sell me a property he didn't own, an antique. Had wonderful presence, sincerity; had me sold, my hand in my pocket. Occurred to me—throughout his pitch, he hadn't once mentioned—" Captain Lorca was standing at the booth.

"Señor Lowry," he said, with a flash of white teeth, "something has come up. May we speak of it?"

"Something about the tractor?" Dan asked.

"No," Lorca said. He bowed slightly toward the Old Man. "You will excuse us a moment, señor?"

Dan stayed where he was.

"Señor Baumgarten," he said, "Captain Lorca."

The Captain and the Old Man greeted each other in Spanish.

"Sit down," Dan said. "Señor Baumgarten is an old friend. Speak freely."

Lorca hesitated, then slid into the booth. The Old Man's face appeared to close itself off from the proceedings. Lorca glanced at him, then spoke to Dan in a muted voice.

"No problem about the tractor," he said. "It is aboard, in good condition. But your passage, señor Lowry—I don't know what I was thinking."

"You were thinking one thousand dollars."

Lorca smiled.

"It was an error, señor, a stupid mistake. The passage will be thirty-five hundred dollars."

Dan finished his drink.

"That's ridiculous," he said.

Lorca shrugged.

"One thousand was too much," Dan said.

"Possibly we could make an arrangement with the tractor—in return for your passage." He glanced toward the Old Man. "And the passage of the señora."

"No," Dan said.

Lorca shrugged again and got on his feet. He was looking at the newspaper on the table. "I am departing tomorrow, ten, eleven o'clock. If your trip is not necessary—"

His hand reached for the paper and drew it in front of Dan. The Old Man blinked slowly.

"I will remove the tractor from my cargo for the five hundred dollars you have already paid," Lorca said.

Dan looked at Lorca's hand, then up at the Captain's face.

"All right," he said. "I have the money, but not with me."

"Tomorrow morning, when you come aboard," Lorca said. "That will be satisfactory."

"All right," Dan said.

Lorca nodded and turned away. The Old Man spoke to him in Spanish and Lorca turned back, frowning. Then his face relaxed around the white teeth. He replied in rapid Spanish, turned and walked away. Dan and the Old Man were silent until Lorca had finished his drink at the bar and gone out.

"You asked him the key question?" Dan said.

The Old Man gazed toward him without expression, then shook his head.

"No," he said. "Just a routine question."

"I'm sorry about the interruption," Dan said. "You were saying—"

The Old Man brushed at the air.

"Not important," he said. "You've placed yourself in the Captain's hands. *Vaya con dios, amigo.*"

Dan looked into his empty glass and pushed it aside with his knuckles. "Thanks for coming. It was a good try."

The Old Man said nothing. Dan got out of the booth and went to the bar. The bartender was a young man with a dark, Indian face and large, brown eyes.

"*Si, señor?*"

Dan gave him some money. "If the gentleman wishes a drink," he said. *"Por favor."*

"*Si, gracias.*"

After Dan had gone, the bartender went to the booth, but turned away without speaking, because the Old Man appeared to be crying. He returned when the Old Man spoke to him, somewhat gruffly, in Spanish, saying, "Is this your home, son? Were you born here in Ensenada?"

"No, sir," the boy said, replying in Spanish. "I was born on a farm in Sonora. I am here in Ensenada only two years."

"I see," the Old Man said.

The boy waited respectfully, but the Old Man was silent.

"Do you wish another drink, sir?" the boy asked finally. "The other gentlemen left money."

"No," the Old Man's head shook stiffly. "No, thank you. Keep the money."

"Thank you, sir."

* * * *

He sat in the truck, drumming on the wheel and staring through the window at the graying sand of the beach, where the fog was drifting in. There was no garage with the house, but there was space to park the truck at one side. It was a graveled area, approached by a roughly paved private road that wound circuitously to the highway. There was a more direct route to the town and harbor that followed the course of the beach, but it was barely passable for motor vehicles and was used only by pedestrians and occasional donkey-drawn carts.

He got down and went into the house by the back door, which led to the kitchen.

Carol was at the sink, washing dishes, moving slowly and without direction. She wore a yellow plastic apron over a blouse and a pair of white panties. Her unkempt hair clung in damp ringlets to her face and neck. She wore no makeup. On the stove, behind her, two potatoes swam in bubbling water. She glanced at him when he entered, then lowered her eyes to her chore.

"Hi," she said.

He nodded and went past her, toward the other room.

"Watch out for the lobsters in the bathtub," she said.

He stopped and looked around at her, but she was intent on the dishwater.

In the bathroom, he looked down at the tub, where two lobsters moved sluggishly in a small amount of murky water. She came to the door in her apron, pushing her hair back from her neck.

"My God," he said.

"A man came by, selling them," she said. "What would I do with live lobsters? But they only cost fifty cents apiece and—I bought them. I thought the man would kill them and fix them and I'd have everything ready when you got home, but he wouldn't, or he didn't understand me."

"Where did you get the water?"

"From the ocean. In a bucket. It took about six trips. I didn't know how much they needed. I worked like hell because I was afraid they might die before I could get the water up here. I ran a little in from the tap, then I decided that water wouldn't be good for them."

He gazed at her and his head moved stiffly.

"Well, how did they get in the bathtub? Did you carry them in?"

"Oh my God no! I wouldn't touch them. The man started to hand them to me, but I screamed and shook my head. So he said something in Spanish—'*donde*,' is that it?—and I made him bring them in and put them in the bathtub. I thought he would throw a fit, laughing. So I gave him a dollar and got rid of him. Then I got the bucket and went for the water."

They watched the two lobsters, which were moving about, close together, brushing into each other and veering away.

"They get along all right," she said. "You suppose they're married?"

He put his arm around her, kissed her face and led her into the bedroom. He pulled her down on the bed and held her tightly, kissing her face and throat, and brushed at her hair with his hand.

"Carol—" he said.

"Yes," she said. Then, "You know, you're an awfully big guy. It's funny, seeing you on the street, you're not so gigantic, but up close— wow!"

"Wow-ee."

"Wow-ee."

He loosened the strings of her apron and pulled it off and unbuttoned her blouse, his fingers moving with unaccustomed quickness, now and then fumbling.

"What about your supper?" she said.

"Supper's for dessert," he said. "*Postre.*"

"*Postre?* I thought that meant 'desert'—like sand."

"So did I once, till a guy set me straight—guy named Tony."

She began to undress him, leisurely at first, teasing, then with sudden urgency, tearing at the fastenings. He embraced her crushingly and she cried out, twisting under him.

"Carol," he said, "I love you."

She seemed to fall away beneath him, so that he raised himself, looking for her.

"Big Dan," she said. "Oh please—do it!"

# CHAPTER 13

She slept while he fixed the lobster, and he woke her slowly. They bathed and dressed for dinner, more formally than usual. She set the table in the living room, so they could look out at the beach. The fog was thin and restless, lifting and settling at random and the glow of the harbor lights was uncertain, fitful. There was a bottle of wine they had bought on their first visit to town and they drank it with the lobster. When the wine was gone, they put a lighted candle in the neck of the bottle.

"What's for *postre?*" he said.

"I don't know," she said. "There's whisky."

"That's fine."

He got the bottle and two glasses from the kitchen and set them on the table.

"Did you see the Old Man today?" she asked, not looking at him.

"Yes."

"How is he?"

"Same as always."

"That tells me a lot."

"I mean, he's sort of a professional wise man. He can't help it."

She sipped at the whisky.

"Did you see Captain Lorca?"

"Yes—I did."

She waited.

After a while he said, "He's sailing in the morning"

"Oh? What time in the morning?"

"Mid-morning."

"Like ten o'clock?"

"Yeah."

She searched his face, its expression elusive by candlelight. "All you need," she said, "is a big, fat cigar."

"I forgot to get some," he said.

He poured more whisky in his glass, then offered her the bottle, but she covered her glass with her hands.

"What did you and Mister Baumgarten talk about?" she said.

"His name is Jack. Jack Baumgarten."

"All right. What did you and Jack talk about?"

"Well, we talked about how nice the weather was and about the fishing around here, and he filled me in on the stuff back home—"

"What stuff?"

"About the weather and the fishing and—"

"Oh shit," she said.

She got up so abruptly that she rocked the table and Dan caught the bottle in time. She picked up a small load of dishes and carried them to the kitchen and he sat on at the table, now and then drinking the whisky, his face knotted and brooding.

* * * *

In the bedroom, she was rubbing lotion on her hands, standing at the window. The fog had thickened and the lights of the town and harbor were diffused and vaguely distant. He had the bottle in one hand and a glass in the other and he poured some whisky into it and offered it to her. She accepted after a moment and drank, turning the glass in her hands. After a minute, she left the window, sat down on the bed, set the glass on the floor and began to take off her shoes and stockings. Dan took a drink from the bottle.

"Little Carol," he said.

She glanced up from an inspection of a bruise on her left thigh.

"You on some kind of a deadline?" she said. "You have to kill the bottle by midnight?"

"Yup," he said.

He leaned over her and she held him back with both hands and slid out from under him to her feet.

"Where's the suitcase?" she said.

He looked around.

"Closet," he said.

She started into the closet and he set the bottle on a chest of drawers and pushed in ahead of her.

"On a high shelf," he said. "I'll get it."

He brought the suitcase out and opened it on the bed. She started pulling out drawers, lifting things out and putting them in the suitcase—a few bits of lingerie, a blouse, the skirts and dress he had bought her first. After a while, he leaned down and picked up the glass, as if fearful she would knock it over. He was holding the glass loosely, waist high, when she said, "What shall I put in for you? Everything?"

He said nothing. She turned and he was standing there with the glass, gazing at her. Her face tightened. She whirled and slashed at his hand, knocking the glass against the wall.

"Talk to me!" she yelled.

She was shaking all over. He gripped her arms tightly and held her till the shaking stopped and she stood stiffly still with her eyes closed.

"Yes," he said quietly. "Come on, little Carol, let me talk to you."

He led her by the hand into the living room. She went along quietly, but when he sat in a large armchair and tried to put her on his lap, she hung back stubbornly.

"Go ahead," she said. "Talk."

He held her one hand, brushed his free hand across his eyes as if to clear them.

"Listen," he said, "it was a crazy idea."

Her small hand clawed its way into a fist inside his large one. "What do you mean? I thought it was all set."

"Carol, listen to me, there's no place to go."

"Yes there is. There is a boat. We know where it is and when it leaves. We know where it's going and we know the man that runs it."

"We couldn't stay there—a few weeks—months. Then we'd have to duck out—go somewhere else."

"I love to travel."

"Listen, the time would come when we couldn't duck out—we'd be broke. When I saw Lorca today, he jumped the price on us."

"He what?"

"From one thousand to thirty-five hundred."

"Why? Why would he do that?"

"Because he knows you're on the run."

"Flow would he know?"

"It's in the paper."

"He's guessing! He doesn't even know my name. Is there a description in the paper?"

"Not much, but what's the difference? So he was guessing—he happened to guess right."

She tried to pull her hand free, but he held her. "So that's it," she said. "The money."

"No, no! I don't care about the money—"

"'I love you,' he says, but not for thirty-five hundred dollars."

He shook his head as if dazed. He released her hand, put his hands on her waist, holding her.

"Dan," she said, "don't make me go back. I can't—" She thrust herself against his face. "Feel that! Tell me it wouldn't make any difference if we couldn't be together for years. It wouldn't matter to you."

"I can't tell you that. Naturally it would matter."

"So you could come and visit me once a month and we could look at each other through some goddam screen or something."

"No," he said. "Shut up now. But, Carol—I don't see any other way." Her fists beat at his shoulders.

"There *is* another way."

"We'll find a good lawyer. Maybe he'll get you off."

"No! Nobody can get me off. I don't have any defense!"

He said nothing and she continued to beat at him with her fists.

"All right," she said, "if you want to be high and mighty about it—all right, I did wrong. I shouldn't have killed him. I owe a debt to society. Goddam it, he asked for it!"

"Shut up now," he said. "It's not a question of high and mighty, right or wrong—it's something else."

"What else?"

"It's something—inescapable. It's one thing you can't run out on. It always was. I don't know why. Maybe it's a natural law."

"Who made it? Who made the law?"

"I don't know."

"People run out on it all the time. You think every—every person that kills somebody gets caught—and punished—all—one hundred percent?"

"Of course not."

"Then why should I be the one?"

"Carol, listen—"

She pulled away from him.

"Listen to what?" she said. "I'm busy."

She went into the bedroom and slammed the door.

He stayed in the chair. There was the sound of her movements behind the closed door, loud and careless at first, fading gradually to silence. He sat there for about an hour and then he went to the kitchen, his tread heavy and slow, and drew a glass of water. There was sweat on his face and he brushed at it with his hand. He took off his coat and tie and opened his shirt. He scratched his chest with both hands, with mechanical, rhythmic doggedness, and finally stopped and looked at his hands, first the palms, then the backs, as if engaged in an absorbing study.

There was a clock above the sink, a green hexagonal box with a white face and black hands. It read half an hour past midnight. He peered at it for some time, drank another glass of water, then sat down in one of the kitchen chairs and took off his shoes and socks. He sat there for a while, inspecting his bare feet, and at one o'clock, he got up and left the house and walked down on the beach. The fog was so heavy now that after half a dozen paces, he was no longer in sight of the house.

\* \* \* \*

In the bedroom, the girl heard the door open and close, and got out of bed and went to the window. She was naked and, after peering out for a minute or two, she began to shiver. She went back to bed, pushing her way feet first under the sheet. The suitcase was still on the bed, with the top down but not fastened. In a sudden fit of temper, she kicked at it and knocked it to the floor, where some of its contents spilled out. She lay on her back with her hands clenched outside the sheet, and after a while she got up, put the spilled garments back in the suitcase, closed and latched it and set it against the wall beside the door. She went to the bathroom and a little later returned and got into bed. She made a faint, whimpering sound and ground her face roughly into the pillow. Pretty soon, she turned onto her back.

"No," she said. "Oh Jesus—no!"

\* \* \* \*

When he opened the bedroom door and looked in, the girl's eyes were closed. He stood near the bed, looking at her, then went to the chest, took down the whisky bottle and left the room. He was in his shirtsleeves and his damp trousers were rolled above his bare ankles.

He was sitting in the big chair, holding the nearly empty bottle in one hand, when she came out of the bedroom. It was about four o'clock in the morning. The light in the room was a yellow patch from the kitchen and she moved in and out of it aimlessly. Her breasts, lightly pendant, swayed with the rhythm of her pacing. She raised her hands to push at her hair and her breasts rose with the gesture and fell softly. At length she approached his chair and stood before him with her hands at her sides. When he came forward, she embraced his head and shoulders, holding him against her. He let go of the whisky bottle and his hands caressed her loins and buttocks.

"Lover," she said. After a while she said, "You want me in a cage somewhere? A steel cage? Or do you want me like this—free—any time you feel like it?"

His hands tightened on her back.

"Carol—" he said.

She wrenched herself out of his hands. Crouching, she backed away toward the bedroom.

"You can't make up your chicken mind?" she said. "All right—*Lorca* does. Lorca wants me. I can go with Lorca anytime. I don't need your thirty-five hundred dollars, or your tractor, and I think if I play my cards right, I can get you back your goddam five hundred dollar deposit. Is that what you want?"

He sat still in the chair, watching her.

"Did you hear me?" she yelled. "I can go with Lorca for free! All I have to do is pick up the suitcase and go."

"All right," he said. "You can go with Lorca."

"Will you try to stop me?"

He shook his head. "No. I won't try to stop you."

She was crouched, trembling, in the bedroom doorway.

"You—chicken!" she said.

He watched her back into the room and the door close. He rubbed his face with his hands, then settled back slowly. His left hand, dangling over the arm of the chair, struck the bottle and knocked it over. He groped, found it and tipped it up over his mouth, then sat with his head back, the bottle dangling from his hand over the chair arm.

After a while he roused and turned his head, listening. There was a knocking and he appeared to have trouble placing it. The knock was repeated and he turned his head till he was looking at the front door. He started up, pushing with his free hand, still holding the bottle, as if his hand were attached to it permanently, then sank back in the chair. The knock came again.

"Come in," Dan said. Then, louder, "Come on in!"

The door opened slowly and Captain Lorca came in. He hesitated, hand on doorknob, till he found Dan in the chair.

"Señor Lowry," he said.

"Hello, Captain."

The Captain wore dungarees, a turtleneck sweater and a pea jacket. His yachting cap was in his hand when he came in and closed the door.

"Excuse me," he said, "I had no other way to reach you—"

"All right, what's the trouble?"

"It is only that I must sail much sooner than I had planned—soon after daybreak, if the fog permits. The harbormaster requires the berth. I wanted to be sure you understood."

"Oh," Dan said. He held the bottle up, squinting through it toward the lighted kitchen. "I regret that I can't offer you a slug, Captain. I just ran out."

"Please don't think of it."

"But I do," Dan said. "I feel like hell about it."

The Captain reached behind him toward the door.

"Don't go," Dan said. "Hang around and fill me in on Guayaquil."

"I must get back to the ship, señor. I have a taxi waiting."

"That's a shame. La señora will regret that she missed you."

"Please give la señora my best wishes—"

The bedroom door opened and Carol came out. She was wearing a skirt and blouse, but her hair was down and she wore no shoes or hose. Dan sat forward, propped on his elbows, looking from Carol to the Captain and back again. Lorca bowed stiffly.

"Señora—"

"Captain Lorca," she said, "there's a change of plans."

"Yes?" Lorca said.

"El señor will not be sailing."

"I see—"

"However, I myself wish to go with you—alone."

After a moment, the Captain shrugged lightly.

"Very well," he said. "If you did not hear, I explained to señor Lowry that the time of departure has been advanced—"

"I heard. I'll be ready."

Lorca bowed and his hand found the doorknob.

"Oh—Captain," Carol said, "I should explain—I can't pay for my passage. I have no money."

Lorca spread his hands.

"Of course," he said. "It is understood. You may board the ship at dockside, numero seventeen."

"Thank you," she said. "There's one other thing, Captain. Señor Lowry would like the five hundred dollars he paid you in advance."

She toyed with the top button of her blouse. Lorca slapped at his trousers.

"But, señora, I am sorry—"

"If he does not get the money," she said, "he may prevent me from sailing."

The Captain stared at her.

"If you will come in here with me, Captain Lorca," she said, pushing the bedroom door wide, "I think we can make an arrangement."

The Captain glanced at Dan, who sat motionless in the chair, then looked at the girl again. She half-turned, moving toward the bedroom.

"El señor is not my husband," she said. "As you probably guessed."
She stared into the room, paused and looked back over her shoulder.
"Well, Captain?"

Captain Lorca, moving wide of the chair but without looking at Dan,
started toward the bedroom.

"No!" Dan said hoarsely.

Rising, he hurled the whisky bottle against the far wall of the room,
where it smashed. Alertly, light and cat-like on his feet, the Captain
turned to come up facing Dan.

"Get on back to your ship, Captain," Dan said.

"Listen—" the girl said.

Lorca watched Dan's face closely. "I have an invitation to remain."

Dan reached for the lapels of the Captain's jacket and Lorca hit him
twice, with fists like rocks, once in the face and once low in the chest.
The girl screamed. Dan fell backward into the chair, clutched at it for
support and collapsed to his knees, holding himself with both arms over
his chest. There was blood on his face and he had difficulty breathing.
Lorca, watching, took off his jacket with deliberation. Dan wiped at the
blood and pushed himself to his feet. Lorca kicked him in the chest as
he rose, then slammed one of the massive fists into the side of his jaw,
knocking him across the room against the front door. The girl put her
hands over her face and turned to the wall beside the bedroom door.

The Captain crossed the room to where Dan, fighting for breath, was
pushing himself up on his hands. Lorca's big hands gripped Dan's belt
and shirt collar to drag him clear of the door. The shirt ripped away and
Lorca, off balance, stumbled backward. Dan drove up into his belly with
his head, his hands reaching for the Captain's throat. Lorca hammered at
Dan's head with both fists, but Dan, clinging to him, stayed on his feet.
His weight bore Lorca back on his heels and, stumbling, trying to regain
his balance, into the wall near the girl, who slid away. Dan's fists beat
Lorca's head against the wall and the Captain fought back with savagery,
driving him off. As Lorca moved out from the wall, Dan twisted suddenly, attacking from the side, and knocked Lorca over the arm of the
chair. Dan moved past him toward the front door.

The girl, huddled with her face in her hands against the wall, began
to shiver when the cold air swept into the room. She looked around in
time to see Lorca throw himself at Dan, who still had one hand on the
door. The sound of the door banging against the wall covered the thudding of bone and flesh, the wheezing, grunting gasps. Dan fell on his face
and Lorca pitched forward over him, then straightened. He drew back his

right foot, aiming for Dan's head, and the girl stopped watching and went into the bedroom.

Dan wriggled upward and Lorca's heavy shoe missed his head and smashed into his clavicle. Dan's arms embraced Lorca's legs, dragging him down, and they were grappling on the floor in the open doorway. In the bedroom, the girl sat in the dark with her hands over her ears.

Lorca kicked and fought his way to his feet, with his back to the open door. He was bleeding at the nose and from his left ear, and a cut had opened under his left eye. As Dan started up, Lorca drew back his right foot, then hesitated, as if he would call for a truce. In the moment of hesitation, Dan hit him in the face, driving him out the door, and followed through.

They fought in the sand, down over the beach toward the surf. The Captain's footing in the heavy shoes was sluggish and uncertain. He fell and Dan dragged him to his feet, then hit him, knocking him backward into the surf. The sky had begun to lighten, but the fog was thick around them and it was black over the water and the sand. Distantly, in the direction from which they had come, the open door of the house was a feeble splash of light, refracted by the fog.

The girl sat now with her hands in her lap, listening, but there was nothing to hear but the surf rumbling. She got up and went to the window and the beach was obscured by the fog. She hugged her breasts with her arms and shivered. She started toward the closet, paused, shifted and picked up the suitcase and opened it on the bed. She pulled a sweater from the suitcase and went into the living room with the sweater over her shoulders. She looked out the open door at the fog, started outside, returned and backed across the room toward the bedroom. Then she heard sounds at the back of the house and after a moment she went into the lighted kitchen, walking on tiptoe on her bare feet.

Outside, through the window over the sink, she saw pale headlights and the vague outline of a taxi drawn up beside the truck. There were sounds of feet and dragging sounds on the gravel. She heard Dan's voice, thick, distorted, speaking quietly: "Hey, amigo. Take the Captain back to his ship."

There were more dragging sounds, the slam of a door. The engine ground to life and she watched the headlights retreat, swing in a wide arc and disappear. She was walking away into the living room when Dan came in by the back door. His eyes were swollen to slits and he groped his way along the shelf to the sink, where he leaned, coughing and spitting.

"Carol," he called.

She came to the kitchen doorway and looked at him and looked away. His hands were bloody and twisted and he spoke thickly out of a broken mouth.

"Listen," he said, "Carol—I'm sorry—didn't know what I was doing—running too fast." His throat filled and he spat blood into the sink. "I tried to use you—to get back." His right hand felt over the shelf, searching. "You have a right—fight for your own life."

His hand found the canister, twisted and the lid went spinning. He turned the can upside down and lifted it, spilling the change and bills onto the shelf.

"Go ahead," he said. "Take what you need. You go." Overcome by a coughing spasm, he leaned low over the shelf, holding his chest tightly with his arms. When it stopped, he looked for her, peering, opened his hands stiffly. "Sorry—I can't drive you now. You can go by the shortcut, a few blocks—maybe find a taxi. Good luck, kid."

His shirt was shreds on his back and shoulders. She moved toward him, as if she would touch him, but he was coughing again, his face turned from her and she went away toward the bedroom.

* * * *

When she came back, he was leaning on the shelf. He had cleaned himself up somewhat. Behind him, it was daylight through the window. There was still fog, but it was thinning and lifting. She was fully dressed and carried the suitcase in one hand and her purse in the other. She stopped in front of him, but he said nothing and after a moment, she went on to the back door, opened it awkwardly with her left hand and started out.

"Carol," he said.

She turned back, looking at him. "Yes?"

"Carol—what was your sister's name?"

Her eyes moved, darting, then fixed on a point behind his shoulder.

"Helen," she said. "Her name was Helen." She looked at his face and looked away. "She was very pretty, before the accident. It was my fault—the accident—not my father's. She was teaching me to drive and I got going fast and she asked me to slow down but I was so smart and—it was my fault. He knew it—Freddie Benedict. After the funny game with the makeup, after I had my fit, he threw it up to me—about the accident. And I guess that's why I…) Her words trailed into silence.

Dan's head dropped forward. He ran his hand over his face and winced. His mouth moved, as if smiling, but it was vague in the cryptic wreckage of his features.

"All right," he said, and looked up at her. "Goodbye," he said. *Vaya con dios.*"

His head dropped again and he pushed away from the shelf toward the living room. The girl stood for some time in the doorway, then left the house, silently except for the crunch of her small feet on the gravel.

# CHAPTER 14

The harbor in early morning was gray but not fogbound. A few gulls soared low over the water, among the trawlers, harbor cruisers and other small boats moored close in; higher over the big freighters farther out. There was no breeze and little sound; a pervasive creaking, an occasional deep whistle; shouts now and then from dockworkers and hangers-on and among the fishermen, local and tourist, putting out in the smaller boats.

Well out, alongside the broad pier, a freighter flew the flag of Panama. Her black hull rode low in the water and there was activity on her decks and dock-side about her. Thin black smoke poured from her stacks, though a loading ramp still thrust from the pier into an opening in her port side.

Some forty or fifty yards out from the landward end of the pier, a cluster of idle dockworkers lounged against a stack of incoming freight. Among them, dressed in slacks, a sport shirt and a long-billed straw cap, was the Old Man. The men were talking among themselves in Spanish, but now and then would include the Old Man, with respect and without undue familiarity. "Yes, old one, it is so." The Old Man's eyes moved slowly, scanning the harbor, the long pier, the freighter, returned again to landward. They were talking about Lorca, *sotto voce*, as in a dirty joke, shrugging, nudging, slyly chuckling. "Big man with the girls, Lorca… Some big girl he must of had last night, eh?… Maybe he tried to go without leaving the money, eh?"

A mimic in the group worked his way center stage, stretched to his full height and beat at his chest roughly. "Big man, Lorca, eh? Tough guy!" He bent suddenly, clutching his belly, hobbled erratically, lifting his feet high, climbing an imaginary gangplank. "Stand back. I can walk aboard my own ship. I am Lorca!" He collapsed face down on the dock. There was raucous laughter.

Nearby, a flock of disturbed gulls took sudden flight. Silence fell over the group as the girl walked out on the pier, carrying the suitcase. She took no notice of the men, and there was no sound among them until she had passed, on her way to the freighter, fifty yards ahead. Then the comedian nudged one of the others. "Eh, *chiquita.* Little one. Somebody Lorca can handle." They laughed.

The Old Man was watching the girl, who walked with a stubborn stride on her small feet, her sandals slapping the plank flooring, her slender legs thrusting below her swaying skirt. The weight of the suitcase lowered her right shoulder and gave a pronounced jut to her hip. On the broad pier, she seemed lost, fragile, like a displaced seabird with a broken wing.

She had covered half the distance to the ship when her pace slowed, the thrust of her legs lost determination. She stopped, looking ahead and upward toward the freighter. After a moment, she went on for several paces, then stopped again. She let go of the suitcase and it fell beside her. She put her face in her hand and sat down slowly, her ankles crossed, her purse dangling from her fingers.

In the belly of the ship there was a rumbling. A man on the dock jumped to one side, as a large tractor moved slowly out of the ship, over the ramp to the dock. The operator maneuvered it clear of the ramp, took off his cap and waved it. There was the blast of a whistle, a grating noise as deckhands withdrew the ramp. From inside, hatches swung to, sealing the ship's side.

The girl rose slowly, picked up the suitcase and started back over the pier. The Old Man moved away from the gang of workers and went to meet her.

"You—" she said.

The Old Man smiled. He took the suitcase from her and they went on together toward the town. The girl began to cry.

"I don't know what happened," she said. "I couldn't—his face—his poor face."

The Old Man raised his free arm and laid one slender, brown hand lightly on her shoulder. After a moment, she put her arm around the Old Man, leaning against him.

"All right," he said. "We'll go see what has to be done."

The back door stood open and the house appeared deserted, but the truck stood where he had left it. The Old Man lifted the suitcase into the back of the truck and led the girl into the house. Through the open bedroom door they could see Dan making a bundle of his clothing, leaning over the bed, his fingers stiff and clumsy. He had cleaned himself up and changed his pants and shirt, but his scarred, swollen face was a grotesque mask. The girl hung back as the Old Man left her. Dan looked at her, straightening, lifting the bundle with one hand.

"Little Carol," he said.

She went to him slowly and he put his arm around her and held her with her forehead against his chest.

"You'll make it now," he said.

"Yes," she said.

The Old Man came to the door.

"Some police came," Dan said. "I told them she'd left, by sea. They'll probably be back."

"Then we'd better get started," the Old Man said.

The girl was clinging to him, her face hidden, and Dan had to turn her to get her started.

"Where?" she said.

"Home," he said. "Everything will be easier in our own country. I have very little Spanish."

They left the house and got into the truck, the three of them, the girl in the middle. On the beach, a gull rose, cutting seaward.

"It was nice here," the girl said.

"Maybe someday we'll come back," Dan said.

"Maybe," she said.

He got the truck started, backed away from the house and turned into the road toward the highway.

"Do you want to go by the hotel and pick up your things?" Dan asked the Old Man.

"No," the Old Man said. "I can send for my things. Unless you want to be alone—I have some Spanish."

"Gracias." Dan said. "Muchas gracias."

"Nothing," the Old Man said.

The girl said nothing, but sat with her hands in her lap, looking straight ahead as they drove.